House of
Several Stories

a tragedy in two acts of nonsense

by A. John Boulanger

A SAMUEL FRENCH ACTING EDITION

SAMUEL FRENCH

FOUNDED 1830

NEW YORK HOLLYWOOD LONDON TORONTO

SAMUELFRENCH.COM

ISBN 978-0-573-70008-8   Printed in U.S.A.   #28065

MUSIC USE NOTE

IMPORTANT BILLING AND CREDIT REQUIREMENTS

HOUSE OF SEVERAL STORIES was originally produced at The Kennedy Center as part of the American College Theatre Festival in May 2009. It was presented by The Search Party in conjunction with Texas State University. It was directed by Jeremy O. Torres. The costume design was by Abbey Moore Graf; the set design was by Vanessa Velasquez; the lighting design was by Chris McKnight; and the sound design was by Daniel Schaetz and Adam Smith. The production stage manager was Lara Willars. The cast was as follows:

MOTHER	Melissa Grogan
BASTIAN	Travis Hackett
RISSA	Ashley Rhodes
ABIGAIL	Ragan Rhodes
THOM	Kenneth Hill

HOUSE OF SEVERAL STORIES on August 6, 2009 at Austin Playhouse (Imagine That Productions). It was directed by A. John Boulanger. The costume design was by Jillan Hanel; the set design was by Griffon Ramsey; the lighting design was by Jason Amato; and the sound design was by Craig Brock. The production stage manager was Jennifer Anderson.The cast was as follows:

MOTHER	Lauren Lane
BASTIAN	Martin Burke
RISSA	Meredith McCall
ABIGAIL	Kelli Schultz
THOM	Adam Pearson

CHARACTERS

MOTHER - 50s, Sue, warm but absent, never without a cocktail
BASTIAN - 30s, adopted brother, optimistically suicidal
RISSA - 30s, sister, skittish, stuck
THOM - 30s, military, a rugged angel, charming with an edge
YOUNG WOMAN/ABIGAIL - 16, mysterious and mature

SETTING

Easton. Home sweet home.

TIME

Thanksgiving, we think.

For Mom.

ACT I: ALL MY CHILDREN

(black out)

(faint sound of a distant wind)

(Whispering voices emerge and envelop the stage. The whispering shifts to chatter; rises in volume; reaches a crescendo; and ends in a single female's laughter. The laughter trails off with the wind. Our play begins.)

(Lights slowly come up on the simple, but elegant, living area of a home. A free-standing window and a door unit separate the playing area from the outside world. Walls are unnecessary. There are no curtains on the window.)

*(**MOTHER** enters, wearing a slip, high heels and pearls. She holds a cocktail glass, which seems a natural extension of her hand. She looks about the room for something to do, but everything seems to be in order. She moves to the sofa, as her gaze falls to a carpeted area. She reluctantly goes to it, kneels, and places her ear to the floor. Nothing is heard, or perhaps something is. She stands, smiles, and heads back to the sofa.*

*(**MOTHER** half-heartedly fluffs a pillow or two before quickly and smoothly reaching into the sofa cushions. She pulls out a flask, refreshes her drink, and places it back into the sofa.)*

*(**MOTHER**'s attention shifts to a bureau, where an open box lay atop it. She warily approaches the box, and without looking at its contents, closes it. She reverently walks it to the sofa, and hides it underneath. Her focus shifts to the window, as **BASTIAN** appears just outside it. They smile.)*

(**MOTHER** *goes to the window, and begins to clean the pane.* **BASTIAN** *waves to gain her attention, but she continues to clean it, as if trying to remove his image from the glass.*)

(*Her focus slowly returns to her carpet. She walks to the spot she placed her ear to before, and empties the contents of her glass onto the floor.* **BASTIAN** *witnesses this, and then heads for the front door.*)

(**MOTHER** *smiles and retreats upstairs.*)

(**BASTIAN** *enters, wearing many layers, ending in a pea coat, and carrying an overnight bag.*)

(*He drops his bag at the door and reminiscently circles the room. He reaches into the sofa, removing* **MOTHER**'s *flask. He smiles, returns it, but in a different spot from where it was before.*)

(**BASTIAN** *rubs his hand through his hair, as if in thought, and then intently walks to the window. He places his oiled hand on the freshly-cleaned pane, leaving his print behind. He looks to the carpet, walks to an area, and kneels. With a thoughtful smile, he addresses the audience:*)

BASTIAN. My father used to weed eat our carpet.

MOTHER. *(entering)* Oh, Thom...

BASTIAN. Oh, Mother.

MOTHER. You aren't Thom.

BASTIAN. That's a relief.

MOTHER. Isn't it?

BASTIAN. I'm Bastian.

MOTHER. My son.

BASTIAN. That's the one.

MOTHER. Then I must be your–

BASTIAN. Mother!

MOTHER. Bastian!

(She rushes to greet him, without ever really touching him.)

BASTIAN. No, you're my mother "Sue." I'm Bastian. Who's Thom?

MOTHER. Who cares? You're Bastian–

BASTIAN. *(echoing)* Who cares I'm Bastian?

MOTHER. My favorite son is home.

BASTIAN. The competition is pretty slim.

*(**MOTHER** wisps through the room and poses on the sofa.)*

MOTHER. I wasn't expecting you until tomorrow.

BASTIAN. It is tomorrow.

MOTHER. So soon?

BASTIAN. Yes. But Mother.

MOTHER. Yes, dear?

BASTIAN. What happened?

MOTHER. To whom?

BASTIAN. The window.

MOTHER. What happened to the wind–? Oh, dear.

*(The sight of Bastian's handprint has drawn **MOTHER** to the window.)*

BASTIAN. Did you fall down or something?

MOTHER. Not that I recall.

BASTIAN. And what the hell is this?

*(**BASTIAN** reaches into the sofa and pulls out a large bottle of scotch.)*

MOTHER. Scotch I think, and mind your language.

BASTIAN. You think?

MOTHER. Perhaps it's bourbon?

BASTIAN. It says scotch on the label.

MOTHER. That's right; we're all out of bourbon. Mystery solved: it's scotch. Now, give me the bottle.

BASTIAN. But you don't drink, Mother.

*(**MOTHER** drinks from the bottle.)*

BASTIAN. You never used to drink.

MOTHER. You never used to cry as a baby.

BASTIAN. I–

MOTHER. Do you remember?

BASTIAN. I remember the stories you used to tell–

MOTHER. Not once.

BASTIAN. About me not crying.

MOTHER. You were the quietest baby anyone had ever seen.

BASTIAN. Or heard.

MOTHER. I always thought–

BASTIAN. Or not heard.

MOTHER. I always thought it was something I was doing wrong–

BASTIAN. What?

MOTHER. You not crying.

BASTIAN. Wasn't it?

MOTHER. I used to cry myself to sleep at night–

BASTIAN.	**MOTHER.**
Because I never would.	Because you never would.

MOTHER. Yes. You do remember.

BASTIAN. Stories.

MOTHER. Do you cry now, Bastian?

BASTIAN. Everyone cries.

MOTHER. At what do you cry?

BASTIAN. Nothing comes to mind.

MOTHER. I wish it would. It really isn't healthy not to cry.

BASTIAN. I'm sure that I cry.

MOTHER. You promise?

BASTIAN. I swear.

MOTHER. I'm glad. Now promise not to swear.

BASTIAN. I swear.

MOTHER. Cheeky bastard. I'm sorry.

BASTIAN. For what?

MOTHER. I should mind my language.

BASTIAN. I should mind my mother.

MOTHER. My son.

BASTIAN. But Mother?

MOTHER. Yes, dear?

BASTIAN. Why're you wearing our curtains as if they were a dress?

(**MOTHER** *realizes she is wearing curtains. She stands, twirls, and poses.*)

MOTHER. They just came back from the cleaners.

BASTIAN. That doesn't make it OK.

MOTHER. I had not a thing to wear.

BASTIAN. Now, neither does the window.

MOTHER. Are you saying I look fat?

BASTIAN. That's all I'm saying.

MOTHER. I'll just go change then. *(beat)* I'll just go change. *(exits)*

(**BASTIAN** *smiles and readdresses the audience.*)

BASTIAN. My father used to weed eat our carpet. Right here in this room as a matter of fact. Not that he would remember of course. But once a week, every week, for years, he swore that the carpet had actually grown–sometimes as much as a whole inch or two. And since the riding lawn mower wouldn't fit through the front door, weed eating was the only logical solution. It was his way of working things out, I guess. My mother was always afraid someone would see him through *this* window, so she made sure curtains were always hung and drawn–which would eventually lead to the carpet's death. According to my father. *(beat)* I was always afraid he would eventually run out of carpet. *(beat)* My sister Rissa–

(**RISSA** *appears outside the window, peering in through cupped hands.*)

BASTIAN. –was always afraid. Of everything.

(BASTIAN, unseen, locks the window and goes to the sofa.)

(RISSA struggles to open the window. After several attempts, she finally gives up. She breathes on the glass, draws a heart shape, and then heads for the front door.)

(She enters carrying a smart-looking hatbox and a Christmas present; dressed incognito: in a trench coat, oversized sunglasses, and a scarf fashioned around her neck and head. BASTIAN reclines on the sofa to "hide.")

(RISSA makes her way to the window, and drops her things below it.)

RISSA. *(to her belongings)* Shhh!

(She stops to look about the room suspiciously, as if being watched. Seeing no one, she unlocks the window and sneaks back out the front door.)

(BASTIAN shifts to hide beside the sofa. RISSA reappears outside the window, peering in through cupped hands.)

(She raises the window successfully and crawls through. Feeling victorious, she dramatically unveils herself from her glasses, scarf, and trench coat.)

(RISSA dances her hat box to the sofa. BASTIAN is now hiding behind it. She removes peculiar items from her box, such as a naked, headless Ken doll and a Blow Pop. She unwraps the candy, places it in the neck hole of the doll, and then devours it.)

(RISSA feels a presence, as BASTIAN glides up and then down just behind her.)

RISSA. *(as Ken doll)* Bastian, what the hell are you doing here?

(A naked Barbie doll pops up from behind the sofa.)

BASTIAN. *(as doll)* What the hell are you doing here???

RISSA. It's Christmas time, and mind your language.

BASTIAN. *(as doll)* It's Thanksgiving.

RISSA. So soon? Why're you up so late?

BASTIAN. *(emerging, himself)* It's 4:30 in the afternoon.

RISSA. Are Mom and Dad asleep?

BASTIAN. Mom is taking off the curtains. And Dad is dead.

RISSA. If you rat on me, I'll tell Dad you found his dirty magazine stash. *(gasp)* Why did Mom take off the curtains?

BASTIAN. They made her look fat.

RISSA. Did you tell her that?

BASTIAN. Somebody had to.

(They high-five each other.)

Why are you sneaking in through the window?

RISSA. You aren't going to tell on me, are you?

BASTIAN. Tell on you for what?

RISSA. If they catch me sneaking in again, I'll be grounded for life.

BASTIAN. You're thirty-five years old.

RISSA. How embarrassing would that be?

BASTIAN. And you don't live here anymore.

RISSA. It's so good to be home! I can't believe I just said that.

BASTIAN. Neither can I.

RISSA. Don't you say a word about Max.

BASTIAN. What is the "word" about Max?

RISSA. Promise you won't tell?

(They join pinkies.)

I was out with him all night.

BASTIAN. Oh.

RISSA. I knew you wouldn't approve.

BASTIAN. He's your husband.

RISSA. Don't you say a word to Mom or Dad. *(pause)* Dad's dead.

BASTIAN. Almost a year.

RISSA. How was the funeral?

BASTIAN. I didn't make it.

RISSA. You little bastard.

(They high-five each other.)

Are you going to tell on me?

*(***BASTIAN*** *smiles, shaking his head "no.")*

Liar! I can always tell when you lie.

BASTIAN. How?

RISSA. I get a slight pang in my right ear and a twitch in my big toe. *(Her big toe moves.) (gasp)* Why do you want to destroy me?

BASTIAN. It's fun.

RISSA. *(huge gasp)* I'll give you my red patent leather pumps.

BASTIAN. Oh, yeah?

RISSA. The ones you've always adored.

BASTIAN. Have I?

RISSA. You'd like that wouldn't you–?

BASTIAN. Would I?

RISSA. My red patent leather pumps?

BASTIAN. The ones I found on the football field?

RISSA. The ones you would sneak into my room to try on–

BASTIAN. That wasn't me.

RISSA. Every time I snuck out to meet Max.

BASTIAN. That wasn't me.

RISSA. He only hit me once. Max. Despite what anyone else might say, he's gotten better about his temper. And I've learned to duck. What size do you wear?

BASTIAN. Nine.

RISSA. Great! The pumps are seven; they're yours if you keep your mouth shut.

BASTIAN. I don't want your shoes.

RISSA. But they're red.

BASTIAN. I know.

RISSA. *(spite)* You're adopted.

BASTIAN. I know that, too. *(beat)* I won't tell.

RISSA. You're my favorite brother.

BASTIAN. I'm your only brother.

RISSA. The competition is pretty slim. But since you're adopted that was a very nice thing of me to say.

MOTHER. *(offstage)* Bastian!

RISSA. *(frantic)* Shit!

BASTIAN. *(fake frantic)* Better sneak upstairs.

RISSA. Before she finds out about Max.

> *(The two begin to scurry about the room.)*

Cause a commotion in the kitchen or something.

> *(BASTIAN hurls a throw pillow toward the kitchen.)*

Wait–! You should hide, too.

BASTIAN. Good thinking.

RISSA. Don't say a word.

> *(RISSA is upstage hiding her face with her hat box. BASTIAN knocks on it.)*

RISSA & BASTIAN. Pinkies!

> *(BASTIAN casually leans against a chair under the window.)*

> *(MOTHER enters, now fully dressed, but masked by the curtains she holds before her.)*

MOTHER. What was that noise?

BASTIAN. A gust of wind knocked over the chair.

> *(BASTIAN kicks the chair.)*

MOTHER. The window's closed.

BASTIAN. It was a large gust of wind.

MOTHER. Must be a southerly.

BASTIAN. I'll put another log on the fire.

> *(MOTHER finds a spot in the room, moves to it, twirls, and poses, revealing a stunning dress. After waiting for a response, that does not come, MOTHER whistles at herself.)*

MOTHER. What, this old thing?

BASTIAN. And you said you had nothing to wear.

MOTHER. I found it in *your* old room. I hope you don't mind. I had to let it out a bit. *(to herself)* Does that mean *I'm* fat?

RISSA. *(hidden)* Yes.

BASTIAN. Yes.

MOTHER. Are you hungry?

BASTIAN. No.

MOTHER. Are you sure?

BASTIAN. Yes.

MOTHER. I can make you some pancakes.

BASTIAN. No.

MOTHER. Blueberries are in season.

BASTIAN. I'm not hungry.

MOTHER. It'd be nice if we had some. But we don't.

BASTIAN. Hopes dashed.

MOTHER. What's that smell?

BASTIAN. Rissa.

MOTHER. Rissa! Get down here!

RISSA. You swore on our pinkies!

MOTHER. I really wish you wouldn't swear.

RISSA. I knew I could never trust you.

> (**MOTHER** and **RISSA** *greet each other formally but awkwardly.*)

MOTHER. Rissa, help me hang these curtains.

RISSA. He's lying, Mother. I was with Abigail all night! Not Max!

> (**RISSA** *begins hanging the curtains.*)

MOTHER. Abigail. That name sounds so familiar.

RISSA. Call Abigail's mother if you don't believe me.

MOTHER. Abigail...

RISSA. Yes! Not Max.

MOTHER. Abigail. Wasn't that the name of your imaginary friend, Bastian? When you were five?

RISSA. She was my imaginary friend first. I'm three years older.

MOTHER. I haven't seen Abigail in years.

BASTIAN. You've never seen Abigail, Mother.

RISSA. You never took an interest in our friends.

MOTHER. It's never too late to try. *(to* **BASTIAN***)* How is she?

RISSA/BASTIAN. Who?

MOTHER. Abigail.

BASTIAN. Imaginary.

RISSA. Stop calling her that!

MOTHER. Abigail, Abigail, Abigail.

RISSA. She goes by Constance now.

BASTIAN/MOTHER. Constance?

MOTHER. Sounds like a loose girl. Really, Rissa. I wish you'd be more discriminating about the imaginary friends with whom you associate yourself.

RISSA. You've never liked my friends.

BASTIAN. You've never had any.

RISSA. *(spite)* Adopted.

BASTIAN. Except for Jacques.

(**RISSA** *gasps.*)

MOTHER. I've a good mind to talk to her imaginary parents, this "Constance".

RISSA. Don't embarrass me, Mother. And she isn't imaginary. I was with her all night.

MOTHER. Imaginary or not, Constance sounds like a loose girl.

RISSA. I didn't imagine it. And I wasn't with Max.

MOTHER. Max?

RISSA. And I'm not lying. He is.

(**MOTHER** *retrieves her flask from the cushions.*)

MOTHER. Bastian, I wish you wouldn't lie. It really is a great embarrassment to this family when you do so.

(**MOTHER** *takes a swig from her flask.*)

RISSA. No more embarrassing than that time he was caught having sex on the school bus by Coach Rice during the senior trip.

BASTIAN. That was you.

RISSA. Oh, shit.

BASTIAN. And it was *with* Coach Rice.

RISSA. You promised you would never tell! He's lying, Mother.

MOTHER. Bastian, promise me that was your last lie.

BASTIAN. I swear.

RISSA. Lie.

MOTHER. Why is there a footprint on the window sill?

RISSA. What size is it? Looks like a nine. Bastian, you're grounded.

MOTHER. These curtains just came back from the cleaners.

ALL THREE. This will never do!

MOTHER. Rissa. Remove them.

RISSA. Wha–! Bu–! Huh–! Why doesn't Bastian have to help? It's clearly his print. *(pointing)* Nine-seven-seven-nine.

(**RISSA** *removes the curtains.*)

MOTHER. I really am happy that all my children have come home for the holidays. It makes me feel all warm and fuzzy inside. Remember that time I made your father's favorite? Rabbit stew. And I forgot to skin the rabbit first? Your father didn't even notice. He simply slurped up every last drop and said, "Mmm. This stew makes me feel all warm and fuzzy inside."

BASTIAN. It did, too.

(**RISSA** *is petrified.*)

MOTHER. *(to* **BASTIAN***)* I really am happy that *all* my children have come home for the holidays. *(pause)* I have to pee.

*(**MOTHER** exits upstairs.)*

BASTIAN. What does she mean "all of her children" have come home for the holidays?

RISSA. *(numb)* I cried for a week when I found out she cooked Jacques Brel.

BASTIAN. He was your best friend.

RISSA. And oh-so soft.

BASTIAN. She said it was an accident.

RISSA. You think Jacques hopped into that pot of boiling water all by himself? He had bad knees! I'm sticking with foul play.

BASTIAN. She was just trying to hide from us the fact that we were so poor.

RISSA. We weren't so poor!

BASTIAN. We ate your pet rabbit.

RISSA. *(gathering her things)* Poor us.

BASTIAN. Poor Jacques Brel.

RISSA. I cried for a week! *(starts to exit the window)*

BASTIAN. Max hit you?

RISSA. Only once. *(beat)* I've learned to duck. And if you tell her I was with him last night, I'll kill *your* best friend (like she killed mine).

BASTIAN. I don't have a best friend. And he's your husband; isn't he?

RISSA. Isn't he? Sorry you couldn't make the wedding.

BASTIAN. The invitation was–

RISSA. It was standing room only and I know how crowds hate you.

BASTIAN. How *I* hate *crowds.*

RISSA. Whatever.

BASTIAN. What did she mean by "*all* her children"?

RISSA. We're both home for Christmas?

BASTIAN. Thanksgiving.

RISSA. Do you smell bourbon?

BASTIAN. I think it's scotch.

RISSA. I wish it were bourbon.

BASTIAN. Mother said we're all out.

RISSA. How tragic.

(a thud from upstairs)

BASTIAN. What the hell was that–?

(BASTIAN *rushes to the foot of the stairs and freezes.* **RISSA** *smiles and addresses the audience.)*

RISSA. One night, when I was sixteen, I snuck out the window to meet Max out on the 50-yard line of the football field. I wore my *red* patent leather pumps and my hair in a French braid–which Bastian had fashioned after I woke him for advice on my outfit. He was better at those kinds of things and, imaginary or not, Abigail was nowhere to be found. I wasn't exactly sure what was going to happen that night, but I remember not wearing panties or a bra. It was cold out, but the breeze was invigorating as I barreled down toward the school, smiling from ear to ear–through clenched teeth to prevent the fluttering butterflies from escaping my stomach. When I got to the field, the gate was chained and padlocked. Without a second's thought, I began to scale the looming fence. Perhaps I was eager. But the hem of my skirt, which was already frayed, because apparently we were poor *(shrugs)*, caught on a link and tore as I made my way down. Being a gymnast, I dismounted fine. But the link must have scratched my leg, because the next morning Mother found a spot of blood on my dress. *(beat)* That night I experienced my first kiss. It tasted like bourbon. The butterflies must've become drunk because the fluttering stopped. Everything stopped. That night I had my first kiss. It tasted like bourbon. That night I also lost my–

BASTIAN. *(shifts)* Red patent leather pumps.

RISSA. Red patent leather pumps. *(beat)* I ran home from the football field, hoping the speed coupled with the wind would wash away the smell of the–bourbon. And

I prayed to God the whole way that Mother was still asleep, or if she wasn't, she wouldn't be able to smell me or the bourbon. And I remember praying for the safe return of my red patent leather pumps. It was that night I was convinced God did exist. When I got to this window, I noticed Daddy in his recliner. I knew it was safe to enter because his favorite show was on and he was resting his eyeballs. But when I stepped into the bush just below the window, I landed on the tail of a skunk! Which must have pissed him off, because he sprayed me with his stink! I had asked God to wash away the smell of the bourbon. And He did. And my red pumps showed up outside my door the following morning. *(beat)* I smelled like a skunk's ass, but I knew there was a God.

(the same thud from upstairs as before)

BASTIAN. *(unfreezes)* What the hell was that noise?

MOTHER. *(entering)* A large gust of wind knocked over a chair.

BASTIAN. Must be a southerly.

RISSA. I'll put another log on the fire.

MOTHER. What's that smell?

BASTIAN. Rissa.

MOTHER. Rissa?

RISSA. It's bourbon.

BASTIAN. It's scotch.

RISSA. I wish it were bourbon.

MOTHER. Me, too; I'm almost out of scotch. How about a mojito? I can make us all a nice pitcher of mojitos.

RISSA. You don't drink, Sue.

MOTHER. You should've told me that before I opened the last bottle of scotch.

RISSA. You never used to drink.

MOTHER. You never used to cry as a baby.

BASTIAN. Um. That was me.

MOTHER. Oh. Yes. Rissa used to cry enough for everybody. Do you remember?

RISSA. I remember the stories.

MOTHER. She never stopped as a matter of fact. I thought it was something I was doing wrong.

RISSA. Probably was.

MOTHER. I used to cry myself to sleep at night, because she never stopped. Finally, I got used to it. In fact–

RISSA/MOTHER. It was the only way I could fall asleep there for a while.

MOTHER. *(beat)* Yes. You do remember.

RISSA. Stories.

MOTHER. Do you still cry, Rissa?

RISSA. Yes.

MOTHER. At what do you cry?

RISSA. Everything.

MOTHER. I'm so glad. Will you help me hang the curtains now?

(**RISSA** *begins hanging the curtains.*)

BASTIAN. The window looks better without them, Mother. It actually brings more light into the room.

RISSA. It'll be dark soon.

MOTHER. What if someone should see in?

RISSA. Yeah, Bastian. What then?

BASTIAN. Who?

MOTHER. You never know.

RISSA. You just never know.

BASTIAN. Nobody is out there. Nobody is looking in.

RISSA. Somebody is always out there.

MOTHER. Somebody is always looking in.

RISSA. Quick, Mother, before someone sees!

BASTIAN. Sees what??

MOTHER. You never know!!

RISSA. You just never know!!

(The phone rings, giving them all a start. **MOTHER** *faints to the sofa;* **RISSA** *hides behind the curtains;* **BASTIAN** *watches the two of them for several rings.)*

BASTIAN. I'll get it.

RISSA. *I'll* get it! It could be Max.

MOTHER. Who's Max?

RISSA. Bastian, you promised not to tell! He's lying, Mother.

MOTHER. Bastian, you promised not to lie.

RISSA. Grounded.

(RISSA leans down to the phone, speaking to it, without lifting the receiver. The phone continues to ring.)

Hello, Max?

BASTIAN. *(to* **MOTHER***)* You've never met Max?

MOTHER. Who?

RISSA. *(shaking the phone)* Are you there? Talk to me, Max. Just talk to me. I know you're sorry for what you did, and I–I'm ready to forgive you. *(to* **MOTHER***)* Isn't that rather adult of me?

MOTHER. *(to* **BASTIAN***)* What did he do?

RISSA. Shh!

(RISSA has shaken the receiver from the phone, releasing the sound of a baby crying.)

Are you crying?

MOTHER. I don't think I'm crying. Bastian, am I crying?

RISSA. He's crying like a baby.

MOTHER. How nice. Bastian never cried like a baby or anything else.

(RISSA cradles the phone.)

RISSA. Do you hear him? He's wailing like a babe. Just like me; right, Mother?

MOTHER. I don't know; bring me the phone.

RISSA. He's so sad. I need my red patent leather pumps!

(RISSA drops the phone and runs upstairs.)

MOTHER. That'll cheer him up. Surely.

(*A* **YOUNG WOMAN (ABIGAIL)** *appears, holding a phone receiver and a bundled-up baby.*)

BASTIAN. *(into phone)* Hello? Max? It's Rissa's brother. Bastian.

MOTHER. Did I ever make that pitcher of mojitos?

YOUNG WOMAN. Hello?

BASTIAN. *(to phone)* Yes.

MOTHER. Did we drink it already?

YOUNG WOMAN. Can you hear me?

BASTIAN. *(to phone)* Yes.

MOTHER. I'll just go make another pitcher then.

BASTIAN. *(to phone)* Can I help you?

MOTHER. I'll be fine. *(exits to kitchen)*

YOUNG WOMAN. Is this the Fuller residence?

BASTIAN. The fullest.

YOUNG WOMAN. 13-0-9 Sunflower Lane?

BASTIAN. As long as I can remember.

(*Baby continues to cry.*)

YOUNG WOMAN. Stop it!

BASTIAN. You stop it.

YOUNG WOMAN. I'm trying. *(to baby)* Shh. There, there now. There, there.

BASTIAN. Can I help you?

YOUNG WOMAN. I don't know. You can help me find– *(She drops the baby.)* *(beat)* Oh, shit.

RISSA. *(entering)* You can help me find my red patent leather pumps; all I could find were my old tap shoes.

(**RISSA** *begins to put on the shoes. The baby cries softly throughout.*)

Is he still crying like a baby?

BASTIAN. I think it *is* a baby.

RISSA. Don't you call Max a baby. He's bigger than you and will kick your ass if I want him to.

BASTIAN. There's a real baby on the phone.

RISSA. Real babies don't use phones. Their fingers are too small and they rarely have anything to say.

BASTIAN. It's somebody *with* a baby.

RISSA. What's Max doing with a baby?

BASTIAN. It isn't Max.

RISSA. What did the baby do with Max???

BASTIAN. It's a lady on the phone.

RISSA. What is Max doing with a lady on the phone?

BASTIAN. It's a lady with a baby on the phone–not Max!

MOTHER. *(entering with mojitos)* How *is* Max?

RISSA. Max who?

MOTHER. I was wondering that myself.

BASTIAN. It's not Max!

MOTHER. Not that I would know who that was either way.

RISSA. Are you sure?

BASTIAN. Shh!

RISSA. Then why the hell am I wearing my tap shoes?

MOTHER. You aren't. Those are Bastian's tap shoes.

RISSA. They were mine first. I'm three years older.

BASTIAN. *(to phone)* Hello?

MOTHER. *(to BASTIAN)* Hi, there. *(to RISSA)* Since you have them on, you might as well do a number.

BASTIAN. *(to phone)* Are you there?

RISSA. What am I? Some sort of show pony?

YOUNG WOMAN. *(into phone)* Yes!

RISSA. Anyway, I'm glad I didn't find my red patent leather pumps. I ran all the way upstairs for some stupid lady with some stupid baby.

MOTHER. What lady with what baby?

YOUNG WOMAN. *(to baby)* Stupid baby.

RISSA. Why are you asking me? Ask Bastian.

BASTIAN. *(to phone)* Are you there?

MOTHER. He's on the phone.

ABIGAIL/RISSA. Yes!

RISSA. With some lady with a baby.

MOTHER. How nice. Babies are so nice to have around for the holidays. That isn't a collect call is it?

BASTIAN. Who are you looking for?

YOUNG WOMAN. Thom? Is that you?

BASTIAN. Thom, who?

MOTHER. You should invite her over, Bass–or at least the baby. Is the baby still crying?

YOUNG WOMAN. Why won't you stop?

BASTIAN. *(to MOTHER)* Yes.

MOTHER. Maybe she could drop him off for a while.

YOUNG WOMAN. I can't do this anymore.

BASTIAN. He apparently won't stop.

MOTHER. How nice is that?

RISSA. Oh, Mother, for God's sake! I can cry, too. Look. *(RISSA starts to cry. And then she starts to tap.)* I can also tap. I bet that stupid baby can't tap.

MOTHER. Rissa, stop calling the baby stupid! We haven't even met him yet.

RISSA. Babies *are* stupid. Have you ever tried having a conversation with one? They're idiots!

MOTHER. But they're so nice to have around for the holidays.

RISSA. Or at a barbecue.

MOTHER. Mojito?

RISSA. Fine. But I'm not doing another tap routine.

MOTHER. That isn't a collect call, is it?

RISSA. I can't hear you, Mother; I'm taking off my tap shoes.

(RISSA runs upstairs. We hear a thud offstage.)

RISSA. *(offstage)* I'm all right.

BASTIAN. *(to phone)* I think you might have the wrong residence.

YOUNG WOMAN. 13-0-9 Sunflower Lane?

BASTIAN. *(to phone)* There isn't a Thom who lives here.

YOUNG WOMAN.   **MOTHER.**

    Of course, there isn't–   Of course, there isn't–

MOTHER. Now, Hang up.

YOUNG WOMAN. I'll be right there.

BASTIAN. What?

MOTHER. Hang up, Bass.

YOUNG WOMAN. I'll be right over.

BASTIAN. *(into phone)* What? Why?

YOUNG WOMAN. I've no where else to go. *(gone)*

MOTHER. Because I don't want a large phone bill from some stupid lady with some stupid baby; now, do I?

BASTIAN. *(into phone)* Hello?

MOTHER. Hi, there.

BASTIAN. She hung up.

MOTHER. First she calls collect, and then she hangs up on you. It's probably best that you didn't invite her over. You didn't invite her over; did you?

BASTIAN. No.

MOTHER. It's probably best.

BASTIAN. But she's on her way.

MOTHER. And she wasn't even invited; how rude. Is she bringing that baby that wouldn't stop crying?

BASTIAN. I assume so.

MOTHER. All is forgiven. What's that smell? Rissa, get down here!

(RISSA enters, wearing bunny slippers.)

RISSA. What did I do now?

MOTHER. Help me tidy up a bit for our guest.

RISSA. Bastian's not a guest.

MOTHER. Just help me tidy up.

RISSA. I can't. I have a blister from doing my tap routine.

MOTHER. I'm not asking you to tidy up with your toes. Just take this into the kitchen. *("this" is anything or everything)*

RISSA. Which way is the kitchen?

MOTHER. Take a right at the window and then a sharp left. You can't miss it.

RISSA. What if I get lost on my way back?

BASTIAN. Follow the sounds of our voices.

RISSA. Say something so I know what to listen for.

MOTHER. "Cry Baby Bunting. Daddy's gone a-hunting– gone to fetch a *rabbit skin*, to put the Baby Bunting in."

RISSA. Oh, Jacques.

(She exits to kitchen.)

BASTIAN. What was *that*?

MOTHER. Must be the scotch.

BASTIAN. Lay off the scotch.

MOTHER. I have, dear. This is a *mojito*.

BASTIAN. *(smiles)* Mother–

MOTHER. I'm so excited about our little visitor; aren't you excited about our little visitor?

BASTIAN. Ecstatic. But Mother–

MOTHER. It's been years since we've had a baby in the house.

BASTIAN. That's true. But Mother, I need to–

MOTHER. This is going to be the best Thanksgiving ever.

BASTIAN. Talk. To. You.

MOTHER. All my children are home and some aren't even mine.

BASTIAN. Mother!!!

MOTHER. *(silence)* Yes, Bastian?

BASTIAN. Before they arrive, there's something I'd like to discuss.

MOTHER. With whom, dear?

BASTIAN. You.

MOTHER. *(beat)* Is it about the carpet?

BASTIAN. What?

MOTHER. I've watered it and watered it; it just doesn't seem to *want* to grow. Is it not getting enough sunlight? Should I remove the curtains, like you said?

BASTIAN. It's not the carpet.

MOTHER. This seems pretty serious. I wish your father was here.

BASTIAN. I miss him, too.

MOTHER. No. He was just better at this "serious-discussion" thing.

BASTIAN. Was he?

MOTHER. Wasn't he?

BASTIAN. I don't remember.

MOTHER. Comparatively?

BASTIAN. I guess he was.

MOTHER. Of course, he was. *(beat)* You look so serious. You look as if someone has just died.

MOTHER/BASTIAN. *(to themselves)* Well...

MOTHER. Are you?

BASTIAN. What?

MOTHER. Dying?

BASTIAN. No.

MOTHER. Am I?

BASTIAN. I don't think so.

MOTHER. You aren't certain?

BASTIAN. I'm certain that's not what I was going to tell you.

MOTHER. I'm so relieved. Well, you're not dying, and I'm not dying. Your father's–

BASTIAN. Already dead.

MOTHER. I guess that leaves Rissa. *(smiles)*

BASTIAN. Nobody is dying.

MOTHER. I wish that were true.

BASTIAN. None of the three of us are dying.

MOTHER. No? No. We're stuck here a while longer, I guess; aren't we? (**MOTHER** *downs her drink.*) Perhaps I should sit down.

BASTIAN. You *are* sitting down.

MOTHER. Then I must be ready.

BASTIAN. *(beat)* I'm a little nervous.

MOTHER. I don't know what you have to be nervous about, dear. You already know what you're going to say, so just say it.

BASTIAN. I've decided. That I'm. G–god, this is hard.

MOTHER. You'll feel better once you get it out.

BASTIAN. I've decided. That I'm going to kill myself.

(**MOTHER** *looks to* **BASTIAN**. **BASTIAN** *slowly turns away from her. The lights blink once, almost undetected. Actors are one second before.*)

MOTHER. *(repeat)* You'll feel better once you get it out.

BASTIAN. I've decided. That I'm going to join the service.

MOTHER. Oh. *(beat)* What service would that be, dear?

BASTIAN. The armed one. The military. The United States military?

MOTHER. Oh. *(beat)* How nice; I've been thinking about joining a gym.

BASTIAN. Is that so?

MOTHER. It's never too late to take pride in one's own appearance.

BASTIAN. A gym?

MOTHER. I know, it's silly. It sounds silly. It's silly. The idea: silly. It's a silly idea. Me? A gym. Isn't that silly?

BASTIAN. A gym.

MOTHER. What do you think?

BASTIAN. I think it's a fabulous idea.

MOTHER. Because I'm fat. I think so, too.

BASTIAN. Fabulous idea.

MOTHER. I think so, too. I'm so glad we had this talk. I'm better at them than I thought. We didn't need Martin after all.

BASTIAN. We never did; did we?

RISSA. *(offstage)* If you guys expect me to follow the sounds of your voices, you're going to have to talk a lot louder!

MOTHER. *(whisper)* I have to pee.

(MOTHER tiptoes to the stairs, grabbing the bottle of scotch on her way.)

BASTIAN. Mother.

MOTHER. *(whisper)* Yes, dear?

BASTIAN. *(beat)* Happy Thanksgiving.

RISSA. *(entering)* Mother!

MOTHER. Yes, Rissa?

RISSA. Where are you going?

MOTHER. To make myself more presentable.

RISSA. For whom?

MOTHER. Some lady with a baby, I suppose. *(exits upstairs)* Perhaps you should do the same.

RISSA. What? Ugh. No fun at all.

(BASTIAN is deep in thought on the sofa. RISSA is in her own world; we hear her thoughts.)

A lady with a baby is just a stupid lady with a baby. Stupid babies. "Babies are nice to have around for the holidays." Yeah? Babies are nice to have with beans and potato salad at a barbecue.

(RISSA laughs maniacally. She quickly snaps out of it. She laughs manically again.)

Or in a stew. How about that, Mother? We can have baby stew for Thanksgiving dinner. *(gasp)* I miss Jacques Brel. *(beat)* Babies. *(beat)* Baby. *(beat)* A baby could be nice. Babies are just what you need when you are home for the holidays. Babies are just what you need...

(RISSA leans back, pushing out her stomach, as if pregnant.)

Bastian, I have something to tell you.

BASTIAN. I have something to tell you.

RISSA. Of course you do. Everything's a competition with you. News flash: I'm three years older; I've something to tell you *first*. But it's very important, so it'll have to wait for Mother.

BASTIAN. What took you so long in the kitchen?

RISSA. I was making the turkey.

BASTIAN. Making the turkey?

RISSA. It's Thanksgiving and we're fresh out of rabbits.

BASTIAN. *You* were making the turkey?

RISSA. I didn't touch the stove.

(*They sit in silence. The silence grows into an uncomfortable paranoia.*)

What the hell are we doing?

BASTIAN. Waiting for Mother?

RISSA. That's right; I have news.

BASTIAN. So do I.

RISSA. I'm older.

BASTIAN. We don't need Mother for my news.

RISSA. Mine must be more important.

BASTIAN. She already knows what I have to say.

RISSA. No, she doesn't.

BASTIAN. Yes, she does.

RISSA. No, she doesn't.

BASTIAN. Yes, she does.

RISSA. No. She doesn't.

BASTIAN. Yes. She does.

RISSA. No, she doesn't!

BASTIAN. Yes, she does!

(**RISSA** *grabs* **BASTIAN**'s *face.*)

RISSA. No! She! Doesn't!

BASTIAN. I already told her my news.

(**BASTIAN** *frees himself.* **RISSA** *takes her aggression out on the sofa.*)

RISSA. You told her your news before you told me your news?

BASTIAN. You were in the kitchen.

RISSA. Making the turkey!

BASTIAN. Without a stove!

RISSA. I don't think you're my favorite brother anymore.

BASTIAN. I don't think you have a choice.

> (**RISSA** *stands up slowly, unpleased.*)

RISSA. Mommy!!! *(to herself)* Where is that wretched woman?

BASTIAN. Getting ready for our guest.

> (*Phone rings. The* **YOUNG WOMAN** *with the baby appears.*)

RISSA. Uncle Clifton?

BASTIAN. Who?

> (**BASTIAN** *lifts the receiver;* **RISSA** *hangs it up. Lights out on* **YOUNG WOMAN**.)

RISSA. What guest?

BASTIAN. The lady from the phone is on her way over.

RISSA. Where?

BASTIAN. Here.

RISSA. Why?

BASTIAN. I don't know.

RISSA. Should we hide?

BASTIAN. I don't see why not.

RISSA. She could be dangerous.

BASTIAN. She could be drunk.

RISSA. What was her name?

BASTIAN. I didn't get it.

MOTHER. *(entering)* Maybe the *baby's* drunk. Did you get the baby's name?

BASTIAN. Did she say it was "Thom"?

MOTHER. *(to herself)* Cheeky bastard.

RISSA. Who is this mysterious lady?

BASTIAN/MOTHER. I've no idea.

RISSA. And you invited her over?

BASTIAN. I didn't invite her anywhere.

MOTHER. I invited the baby; I don't care much for the lady.

RISSA. She's coming.

MOTHER. Well, someone has to pay for the baby's cab.

RISSA. No one ever pays for my cabs.

BASTIAN. I'm not sure we even have cabs in Easton.

MOTHER. The baby can't drive himself.

RISSA. That'd be a big baby.

MOTHER. And if he walks, he'll be too tired when he gets here. And a sleeping baby is no fun at all.

RISSA. Maybe that wasn't a lady on the phone.

MOTHER. Maybe it *was* Max.

RISSA. Max who?

MOTHER. I've no clue.

BASTIAN. It was a lady. She had a baby. And she's on her way over.

RISSA. And you're not afraid?

BASTIAN. I've no reason to be.

RISSA. Perhaps. *(beat)* Perhaps it was just Aunt Ruth, playing a trick on us.

MOTHER. What is your Aunt Ruth doing with a baby?

BASTIAN. We don't have an Aunt Ruth.

MOTHER. Oh.

RISSA. Then who am I thinking of?

MOTHER. Your Aunt Barbara.

RISSA. Oh.

BASTIAN. We don't have an Aunt Barbara.

MOTHER. Then who am *I* thinking of?

BASTIAN. I've no idea. We don't have any aunts as far as I know.

RISSA. I think he's right.

MOTHER. It's probably best. Neither your Aunt Barbara nor your Aunt Ruth ever sends cards or gifts around the holidays.

RISSA. Maybe they're poor, too.

MOTHER. You were always better at remembering those kinds of things, Bastian.

RISSA. What was I better at, Mother?

MOTHER. Origami.

RISSA. What the hell is Origami?

(**MOTHER** *makes her way to the carpet.*)

MOTHER. Do you remember how your father and I used to—

(**RISSA** *and* **BASTIAN** *begin a slow-processed fit, a toddler tantrum.*)

RISSA/BASTIAN. I remember. I remember. I remember! I remember! I remember!!!

(**MOTHER** *is lost in a memory.* **RISSA** *and* **BASTIAN** *peak and then freeze.*)

MOTHER. I remember. *(to audience)* When I was fifteen, Martin Fuller walked up to me during homeroom and told me that we were going to the Spring Dance together. And instead of waiting for a response, he simply walked away. I'm sure I would have said, "Yes," but since it wasn't a question, there really wasn't a reason for me to come up with an answer. Which is probably best, because I'm incapable of making decisions on my own. Even when I do, it's invariably the wrong one.

RISSA/BASTIAN. *(shift; softly)* Yes.

MOTHER. I'm certain I would have said, "Yes." Had there been an actual invitation. *(beat)* Two and a half years later, Martin walked me home after the Homecoming Dance, and when we reached the front porch, he let me know that we had been dating for two years and that I was going to marry him after graduation. I remember him trying his best to get the ring around my finger, when he said he must've bought it a size too small. I said, "No. I must've been born a size too large." He finally gave up, and just handed me the ring. And then he started in on how he was going to provide for me, and take care of me and some other business about love. I think. But I couldn't stop thinking about that lime green taffeta dress Priscilla Jackson wore to the dance, and how she glowed when the crown went atop her head. And wishing I had worn a lime green taffeta dress, and wishing that Glenda Barnes had won Homecoming Queen, because at least she was still a virgin. And then I started to cry. Which must have made Martin feel uncomfortable, because he quickly left. After he was gone, I walked home. I didn't have the heart to tell him that he pseudo-proposed to me on the neighbor's front porch. He already seemed so nervous. Perhaps he was drunk. (beat) But as I lay in bed that night, I remember thinking, "Aren't I fortunate?" To have someone like Martin in my life to help me make big decisions about dances and marriage? Since I'm incapable of making decisions on my own. Even when I do, it's invariably the wrong one.

RISSA/BASTIAN. *(shift; softly)* Yes.

MOTHER. I'm certain my answer would've been, "Yes." Had there been an actual proposal.

(**RISSA** *and* **BASTIAN** *come to life.*)

Do you remember how your father and I used to make up relatives who lived in far-off, exotic places?

BASTIAN/RISSA. To give us a better sense of familial connection.

MOTHER. You do remember.

RISSA. My favorite was always Uncle Clifton.

BASTIAN. I almost forgot about Uncle Clifton.

MOTHER. How could you forget your Uncle Clifton?

RISSA. He lived in Malaysia!

BASTIAN. With his eight children and their *au pair.*

RISSA. Jesus H. Macy! Eight children...

BASTIAN. Can you think of anything more tragic?

MOTHER. Two.

BASTIAN. I remember their eight names.

RISSA. I remember their eight names first; I'm three years older.

MOTHER. How could you forget? They're your cousins.

RISSA. In order: Merle, Michelle, Guy, Timothy, Ferrel, Jonathan, Benji, and Melissa.

BASTIAN. I thought Benji was the youngest.

RISSA. That was in order by height. Melissa was dwarfish; wasn't she, Mother?

MOTHER. I thought the *au pair* was a dwarf.

RISSA. Sybil couldn't be a dwarf and look after eight children all by herself.

MOTHER. Of course not. That's why they were all eaten up by tigers, while visiting the National Zoo in Kuala Lumpur.

BASTIAN. Dad said they died of consumption.

MOTHER. Your father had little flair for fiction.

RISSA. What did he have a flair for?

MOTHER. Landscaping.

RISSA. That's right; look at the carpet.

(They all do.)

*(**MOTHER** pours a bit of her drink onto it.)*

What did I have a flair for, Mommy?

MOTHER. Origami is all I recall.

RISSA. *(to **BASTIAN**)* What the hell is that?

BASTIAN. Mother. Rissa has news!

MOTHER. What is it?

RISSA. Why are you asking him? It's my news, and I think you should sit down.

MOTHER. Oh. I thought I was. *(sits)* If this is about Bastian joining the service, I've already heard, and I think–

RISSA. Not everything is about Bastian, Mother. *(quickly to* **BASTIAN***)* What service are you joining?

MOTHER. Was that a secret?

RISSA. The Secret Service?

BASTIAN. The military. The United States military. The navy to be exact.

   *(**MOTHER** and **RISSA** smile, then chuckle, and then laugh uproariously.)*

MOTHER. *(recovering)* Bastian, I've been thinking; this group you want to join?

BASTIAN. The navy.

MOTHER. Are you sure they take people like you?

BASTIAN. What does that mean, "people like me"?

RISSA. *(stops laughing)* Adopted.

MOTHER. Your *age*.

RISSA. Oh.

BASTIAN. "Don't ask, don't tell."

MOTHER. Surely they have ways of figuring it out. They'll probably ask for a birth certificate, and if they have a calculator, they can simply do the math.

BASTIAN. I'm thirty-two.

RISSA. When did you get so old? *(to **MOTHER**)* How old does that make you??

BASTIAN. The cut off age is thirty-four.

RISSA. How old am I again?

   *(**MOTHER** looks to **BASTIAN**.)*

BASTIAN. Thirty-five.

MOTHER. Thirty-five, dear.

   *(**RISSA** faux faints to the floor.)*

BASTIAN. I can still enlist, but I'm running out of time.

RISSA. Wait! Does that mean I can't join the service?

MOTHER. Did you want to?

RISSA. I'd at least like the option. If Bastian gets to join, why can't I? I'm three years older.

MOTHER. I think we've established that as the reason.

RISSA. I don't like that one bit. I think I'll file a complaint.

MOTHER. I think I'll file my nails. Has anyone seen my emery board?

(*RISSA gets a pad and pen from the bureau, handing* **MOTHER** *an emery board.*)

RISSA. To whom should I address the letter?

MOTHER. Clark Gable.

RISSA. Who the hell is Clark Gable?

MOTHER. Very well, address it to me. I always enjoy receiving your letters. There's a stamp in the bureau.

RISSA. I've never written you a letter.

MOTHER. That's right you haven't.

RISSA. In fact, I've never written a letter at all.

MOTHER. Don't you think it's about time you did?

RISSA. I'm too busy, Mother. I'm trying to change the world.

(*RISSA goes to the phone.*)

MOTHER. Oh, Rissa–

RISSA. Oh, Sue. Who's in charge of the United States military?

MOTHER. Activism is so unlady-like.

BASTIAN. The President.

MOTHER. What will the neighbors think?

RISSA. The curtains are hung. *(at phone, without lifting receiver)* Hello, Rosie, I'd like the President of the military, please.

BASTIAN. The United States.

RISSA. He's also the President of the United States. *(confused)* Business or residence?

MOTHER. *(to phone)* He lives in a white house on a hill.

RISSA. Residence.

BASTIAN. You can't just call the White House!

MOTHER. It's so unlady-like.

BASTIAN. *(lifting receiver)* You're not even on the phone!!!

RISSA. *(to* **BASTIAN***)* You just don't want me to kill more people than you when I'm in the military. *(to phone)* Yes, that's what I said. *(to* **BASTIAN***)* Everything's a competition with you. *(to phone)* No, this isn't a joke. Doesn't he have a secretary or someone with whom I can leave a message?

MOTHER. I hate seeing my little peanuts get their hopes dashed.

RISSA. *(to phone)* Don't you dare tell me to have a nice day!

MOTHER. *(smiles)* I really do.

RISSA. She hung up on me.

MOTHER. Are you going to cry?

BASTIAN. I think the military–!

MOTHER. It might make you feel better.

BASTIAN. Is exactly what I need to–!

MOTHER. Come on, Riss.

RISSA. I so wanted to join. Max would've really liked that.

> (**BASTIAN** *begins to have a physical fit (in anger) from being ignored, which continues for some time, and then goes completely unnoticed.*)

Why couldn't you have adopted Bastian before giving birth to me? That way I'd be younger and be able to join the service and make Max happy.

MOTHER. Whoever the *hell* that is.

BASTIAN. *(to* **MOTHER***)* Language! *(to* **RISSA***)* How would that make Max happy?

RISSA. Max was in the military himself. Are you trying to steal him from me?

MOTHER. First Abigail; now Max.

BASTIAN. Max wasn't in the military.

RISSA. Why would I lie?

MOTHER. If anyone else lies today, they're grounded!

RISSA. His heroism was part of his appeal. He fought in the Vietnam War, the Korean War, and that war in the gulf. The Cold War was excruciating on his rheumatism.

MOTHER. I imagine it would be.

RISSA. He also served in *both* World Wars, the French *and* Indian wars, *and* the War on Drugs.

BASTIAN. And he also hit you.

MOTHER. Riss?

RISSA. He has seven purple hearts and two green thumbs like Daddy.

MOTHER. Max hit you?

RISSA. Only once.

BASTIAN. She's learned to duck.

(**MOTHER** *takes a swing at* **RISSA**, *who of course ducks.*)

MOTHER. I guess serving in so many wars must've had an amplifying affect on his aggression level. But still, hitting you is unacceptable. Maybe I should speak to his imaginary parents, too.

RISSA. Don't embarrass me, Mother. And he isn't imaginary. I was with him all night.

MOTHER. I thought you said you were with Abigail all night.

BASTIAN. Constance.

MOTHER. That loose girl???

RISSA. I lied.

MOTHER. You're grounded!!! Go to your room.

RISSA. *(to* **BASTIAN***)* I knew I could never trust you.

BASTIAN. You can't ground her.

RISSA. Not if I run away she can't.

(**RISSA** *jumps up to gather her things.*)

MOTHER. I have no other choice, Bastian. She told a lie.

RISSA. Cause a commotion in the kitchen or something.

BASTIAN. She's thirty-five years old.

MOTHER. Is that the cut-off age?

RISSA. I'm running away with Max! And you'll never see us again!

BASTIAN. She just didn't want to upset you.

MOTHER. Upset me about what?

RISSA. And I'm taking my red patent leather pumps! *(runs upstairs)*

BASTIAN. Maybe *that's* part of her news.

MOTHER. I don't know how much more news I can handle. *(hiccups)* Or mojitos.

BASTIAN. Let's move away from the mojitos.

MOTHER. What'd you have in mind?

RISSA. *(entering)* All I could find were my old tap shoes.

MOTHER. Bastian's old tap shoes!

(RISSA drops the tap shoes in disdain.)

BASTIAN. How about some coffee?

MOTHER. How about a dirty martini? Why don't you whip us up a nice batch of dirty martinis?

RISSA. Dirty martinis? Woo hoooooo! *(quick)* No; I'm running away.

BASTIAN. I'll make us all martinis after we hear her news.

RISSA. Don't you dare try to stop me!

BASTIAN. But you haven't told us your news.

RISSA. That's right; I haven't! *(to MOTHER)* Am I still grounded?

(MOTHER nods.)

(to herself) Yes! *(goes to sofa)* I thought we were having martinis.

MOTHER. That's the only reason I'm still here.

BASTIAN. Rissa. News.

RISSA. I don't know how you're going to take this.

MOTHER. Easier with a martini.

RISSA. I'm pregnant. *(beat)* I'm going to have a baby. *(beat)* I'm going to be a mother, just like you. And you're going to be a grandmother, just like...Grandmother? And Bastian will be an uncle, like Uncle Clifton, and move to Malaysia, thank god. And we'll all live happily ever after and I helped. *(beat)* What do you think?

(MOTHER and BASTIAN smile, then chuckle, and then laugh uproariously.)

BASTIAN. Pregnant.

MOTHER. I thought you were joining the service.

RISSA. I was, but–

MOTHER. The military is hardly the place to have or raise a child. What if he grows up aggressive and hits you like Max?

RISSA. I'm not joining the service anymore, Mother. That was a silly, childish dream. I'm all grown up now. I'm pregnant.

MOTHER. I see.

RISSA. Now, we won't have to have that stupid lady over with her stupid baby.

BASTIAN. Stop calling the baby stupid. You haven't even met him.

MOTHER. Why? Are you going to have your baby today?

RISSA. I'll certainly try. *(She literally tries.)*

MOTHER. We'll just have to see which baby arrives first.

RISSA. But mine will be your grandchild. He should be your favorite.

MOTHER. If he cries the loudest, he will be. You better get a move on, Riss; that lady should be here any minute. Which reminds me, I should check on the turkey.

BASTIAN. Rissa took care of the turkey.

*(**MOTHER** is stopped in her tracks.)*

MOTHER. Rissa took care of the turkey?

BASTIAN. She didn't touch the stove.

MOTHER. Bastian, I think it's time for those martooties.

RISSA. Why can't you just be happy for me? It's not like Bastian's ever going to provide you with grandchildren.

BASTIAN. Why's that?

RISSA. People like you can't have babies.

BASTIAN. We can't?

RISSA. Sure, you can adopt, but do you really want to subject a child to that kind of psychological nonsense?

BASTIAN. What do you mean, "people like me" can't have babies?

RISSA. You're a boy! You don't have a uterus. *(pronounced utter-us)*

MOTHER. Fact of life.

RISSA. If you want to file a complaint, address the letter to Mother Nature.

MOTHER. There's a stamp in the bureau. But, Rissa. I've been thinking; this child that you're having?

RISSA. Jacques? What about him?

MOTHER. Well, peanut. I don't want to dash your hopes again, but–

RISSA. But what?

MOTHER. I thought we had this discussion years ago.

RISSA. What's wrong with my baby, Mother?

MOTHER. Sweetie. You can't get pregnant.

> *(**MOTHER** and **BASTIAN** look to **RISSA**. **RISSA** slowly looks away. Lights blink. It is [once again] one second before.)*

RISSA. *(repeat)* What's wrong with my baby, Mother?

MOTHER. Sweetie, you can't get pregnant. Unless you're married.

BASTIAN. Fact of life.

MOTHER. Mother Nature.

BASTIAN. Stamp's in the bureau.

RISSA. Oh, Mother. I know you can't have babies unless you're married.

MOTHER. It has to be to a man.

RISSA. I know that, too. *(to **BASTIAN**)* You haven't told her?

BASTIAN. Pinkies.

MOTHER. Told me what?

RISSA. That's why I have Max.

MOTHER. Oh, I see. So, Max is...?

BASTIAN. Her husband?

> *(**RISSA** flashes a ring in **MOTHER**'s face.)*

RISSA. I cried when he put it on.

MOTHER. I'm so glad. *(beat)* Why is it on your pinky?

RISSA. He bought it a size too small. I heard that happens sometimes.

MOTHER. Maybe you were born a size too large. That happens sometimes, too. *(beat)* I don't know what to say.

RISSA. "Congratulations"?

MOTHER. Sorry I didn't make the wedding.

RISSA. That's OK. It was a small elopement at the courthouse.

BASTIAN. I thought it was standing room only.

RISSA. There was a lot going on in court that day.

MOTHER. Congratulations.

RISSA. So you're happy with me?

MOTHER. Of course.

RISSA. Then why are you crying?

BASTIAN. Must be the scotch.

RISSA. She should drink bourbon.

MOTHER. We're all out.

RISSA. Bastian, quick with the martinis.

MOTHER. Your father cried every time he drank scotch. He tried to hide it from you as best he could.

BASTIAN. He did a great job.

RISSA. Daddy drank bourbon.

MOTHER. I never knew the difference.

BASTIAN. Neither did he.

RISSA. I did.

MOTHER. *(beat)* Well. I guess it's my turn.

BASTIAN/RISSA. Your turn?

RISSA. Ow! I just felt the baby kick. Look, Bastian.

BASTIAN. He must be doing a tap routine.

MOTHER. It's my turn, now–

RISSA. Oh, Mother. You can't tap.

MOTHER. To share with you *my* news.

RISSA. Can't it wait until Jacques is done with his routine?

BASTIAN. Should I put on some music?

RISSA. Ow! Jacques just did a chug-shuffle and then a riff-drop. Now, *I* have to pee. Hold the news. *(exits to stairs)* Hold. The news. *(gone)*

MOTHER. Why on earth would you want to join the military? Are you angry about something?

BASTIAN. I need to do something with my life.

MOTHER. End it. *(beat)* If you join the military, you're just going to get shot or blown up. If you get shot or blown up, chances are you'll die. If you die, they'll just end up sending you back here, and then I'll have to deal with the mess.

BASTIAN. And what would the neighbors think?

MOTHER. You're better off just joining a gym. *(beat)* Why are you so unhappy? Why do you seem so sad all the time?

BASTIAN. My best friend died last week. My only friend actually.

(There is the longest pause.)

MOTHER. You aren't going to make those martinis like you promised. *(exits to kitchen)* Are you? *(gone)*

*(**RISSA** rushes in from upstairs. She is now, what appears to be, about three months pregnant; maybe a throw pillow?)*

RISSA. I still can't find my red patent leather pumps, but I'm getting closer. *(crosses to window)* Mother, there's a man in your bed! Oh, my Jesus. If I get any bigger; I'll have to sneak in through the back door from now on.

BASTIAN. How tragic. What did you say about a man?

RISSA. There's a man in Mother's bed.

*(**MOTHER** enters with a martini service.)*

MOTHER. What were you doing in my room?

RISSA. Looking for my missing pumps. For which I'm holding you both suspect.

MOTHER. What have I told you about going through my things?

RISSA. *(to* **BASTIAN***)* I think the dirty magazine stash is really hers.

BASTIAN. Who is the man in Mother's bed?

RISSA. I didn't get his name, but he's dressed like a crossing guard.

MOTHER. She's always telling stories.

BASTIAN. Is there a man in your bed dressed like a crossing guard?

MOTHER. Like a navy seal; and no, there isn't.

(**BASTIAN** *goes for the stairs.*)

Bastian!

RISSA. *(mock)* Bastian!

(**BASTIAN** *stops.*)

MOTHER. Dirty martini?

RISSA. I'll take his.

(**BASTIAN** *goes for the stairs.*)

MOTHER. Bastian!

RISSA. *(mock)* Bastian!

(**BASTIAN** *stops.*)

MOTHER. Help me remove the curtains; we need more light in the room.

RISSA. It'll be dark soon.

(**BASTIAN** *goes for the stairs.*)

MOTHER. Bastian!

RISSA. *(mock)* Bastian!

BASTIAN. What???

MOTHER. Where are you going?

BASTIAN. Why is there a man in your bed?

RISSA. And not mine?

MOTHER/BASTIAN. You're "married"!

RISSA. Oh, that's right.

(**MOTHER** *over-dramatically staggers about the room in preparation to faint; or maybe it's a heart attack. She pulls the curtains down in the process.*)

MOTHER. I didn't know where else to put him. I–I–I was waiting for the right moment to...tell...you...

(**MOTHER** *has fallen to the floor. And died.* **RISSA** *and* **BASTIAN** *remain unfazed.*)

RISSA. She always had a flair for the dramatic.

BASTIAN. Are you dating again?

MOTHER. *(undead)* What?

RISSA. Eww.

MOTHER. No.

RISSA. Eww.

MOTHER. I'm a married woman.

RISSA. I thought Dad was dead.

BASTIAN. Who is the man in your bed?

MOTHER. It's not a man.

RISSA. If that wasn't a man, she's one masculine woman.
     (gasp) Mother's a lesbian.

BASTIAN. Rissa!

RISSA. It happens all the time with women her age after their husbands die. He is dead, isn't he?

MOTHER. Your father's dead. And it isn't a man.

RISSA. Lezbo.

MOTHER. It's your brother.

BASTIAN. What?

RISSA. *(to* **BASTIAN***)* Lezbo! *(to* **MOTHER***)* What??

MOTHER. Your brother. Is upstairs.

(**RISSA** *hiccups.*)

All my children are home for the holidays.

(Silence)

RISSA. *My* brother is *upstairs?*

MOTHER. Yes, Rissa.

RISSA. Then who the hell are you?

BASTIAN. Your brother.

RISSA. Liar! Mother, he's lying. Ground him, whoever he is. *(exits upstairs)* I'm coming, Bastian! I'm coming. You can help me find my red patent leather pumps!

BASTIAN. I'm Bastian!

RISSA. Lies! *(gone)*

(We hear a thud.)

(offstage) The baby's all right!

*(**MOTHER** and **BASTIAN** share a look.)*

BASTIAN. Who is upstairs?

MOTHER. Your brother. Thom. *(exits to stairs; stops; smiles)* Thom. *(gone)*

(Doorbell rings. A baby cries. A knock.)

*(**BASTIAN** looks to the front door, then to the stairs, then to the audience.)*

(Lights begin to fade.)

*(**BASTIAN** places the curtains over his head and curls up on the sofa.)*

(Blackout)

END ACT I.

ACT II: FISH BABY

(Lights fade in.)

*(**BASTIAN** emerges from the curtains on the sofa. He tilts his head back and exhales. He smiles, opens his eyes, and addresses the audience.)*

BASTIAN. My best friend died last week. And for some reason I've been totally incapable of crying. Actually, he was my one and only friend, but still I've yet to shed one tear. When I went to the funeral, I didn't want his other friends and family to think I was heartless, so I faked it. I over-compensated by trying to look like I was crying, and I ended up wailing loudly and uncontrollably. With an occasional body writhe. Which must have looked more like mockery than sincerity, because I was asked to leave the funeral. It's probably best; I was already twenty minutes late for work by that point. I ended up losing that job two days later for spilling an extra-hot, quad-tall, two-pump, no-whip, non-fat, four-Splenda mocha all over a coworker. I told the manager it was an accident, but he refused to believe me since the coworker was on the other side of the room from where I was when the extra-hot, non-fat, four-Splenda mocha spilled. He also said it was because I had spilled two extra hot lattes twice before on that same coworker. It's his job to keep production cost down. So I was fired. I've never been able to keep a job for more than a month. His last words to me were, "You should take an anger management course." Which puzzled me. Because I've never been angry a day in my life. I don't think I've cared enough about anything to get angry. Maybe I haven't cared enough about anything to cry yet either. Wouldn't that be tragic? Wouldn't that be sad? *(pause)* Apparently, not sad enough. So. I smile. *(beat)* I bet he was smiling, too. When he pulled the trigger. My best friend. Alex.

(A knock at the door.)

*(**MOTHER** rushes down the stairs, in a lime-green taffeta dress. And a tiara. She goes to the center of the room; twirls; poses; and whistles.)*

MOTHER. Rissa has locked herself in my room. I hope she isn't going through my things. I borrowed this from your closet; I hope you don't mind. Wasn't there a knock at the door?

BASTIAN. No.

(There is a knock at the door.)

MOTHER. Why are you being rude to our guest?

BASTIAN. Maybe we should dispense with the guests due to the recent discoveries in our personal family business.

MOTHER. I have no idea what you just said.

BASTIAN. What about this Thom character?

MOTHER. Rissa is in there with him. How much damage can she do?

BASTIAN. I'd like to meet him.

MOTHER. As soon as she unlocks the door, I'll prepare him for a presentation.

BASTIAN. Presentation?

MOTHER. He's still in bed.

BASTIAN. Shouldn't you explain to us how he came to be our brother?

MOTHER. As soon as Rissa comes down, I'll explain everything.

*(**MOTHER** tries to pass **BASTIAN**, but he grabs her forcefully by the arm. There is an odd tension.)*

You're right about the curtains. It brings more light into the room this way. It'll be good for the carpet.

BASTIAN. What if someone should see in?

MOTHER. Who?

BASTIAN. You never know.

MOTHER. Nobody is out there. Nobody is looking in.

(There is a tap at the window. It is **YOUNG WOMAN** *with baby in hand.)*

Don't be rude to our guests, Bastian.

*(***MOTHER*** goes to the window and opens it.)*

Well, what have we here?

*(***MOTHER*** takes the baby from the* **YOUNG WOMAN** *and closes the window.)*

It's a baby. Baby boy. Yes, it was. It's a big baby, baby boy. With big baby boy feet, and big baby boy hands, and toes, and a nose, and eyes, and a big baby boy belly. I'm going to eat that belly. Yes, I am. Arr, arr, arr. *(beat)* Arr, arr, arr. *(beat)* This baby isn't responsive to my coos. He hasn't cried, spit or gurgled once. He isn't dead, is he? I'm not holding a dead baby, am I?

YOUNG WOMAN. *(entering front door)* He's finally asleep.

MOTHER. His eyes are open. What is he a fish? Is that what you are? A big baby boy fish? Yes, you are. A big fish baby with big brown fish eyes. *(no response)* This is no fun at all.

*(***BASTIAN*** is wary of the* **YOUNG WOMAN***;* **MOTHER** *pays no attention to her.)*

YOUNG WOMAN. It's the first time he's stopped crying since we left the hospital.

MOTHER. How nice is that? You didn't make him walk all the way over here, did you?

YOUNG WOMAN. It was only twelve blocks. I did the walking.

BASTIAN. Twelve blocks?

YOUNG WOMAN. From the pay phone by the football field.

MOTHER. You should have brought him over in a cab. He's all worn out now. He'll probably never cry.

YOUNG WOMAN. I don't have money for cabs.

BASTIAN. I'm not sure we even have cabs in Easton.

*(**MOTHER** raises the baby above her head.)*

MOTHER. Ah-boo!

(No response. She bounces him slightly.)

Ah-Boogety, boogety, boogety, boo!

(Still no response.)

No fun at all. I guess we'll just have to wait for his second wind. *(shakes him violently)* He's so sleepy. I hope he cries at least once before dinner. I bet if we don't feed him, he'll get hungry. And hungry babies love to cry. That's what we'll do. We'll not feed you. Speaking of crybabies: Rissa–!

*(**MOTHER** finally notices the **YOUNG WOMAN**; she is completely at a loss for words.)*

(unsure) I should go check on Rissa's turkey. Do you mind if I take him into the kitchen?

YOUNG WOMAN. Take him.

MOTHER. I bet he'd like to play with Rissa's turkey. Wouldn't you fishy, fishy baby? *(exits)* Why won't you cry? *(gone)*

BASTIAN. Mother, don't forget we still have family–!

*(There is an awkward silence–a familiarity, an uncertainty. **YOUNG WOMAN** crosses the room, as **BASTIAN** counters her position. They square off.)*

I should go check on my sister. Or my new brother. That might be easier to deal with after you leave. Can I take your coat?

YOUNG WOMAN. And do what with it?

BASTIAN. Lay it across this chair.

YOUNG WOMAN. I'm not staying long.

BASTIAN. You're not leaving–

ABIGAIL. You going to stop me?

BASTIAN. Until she hears that baby cry.

ABIGIAL. Who?

BASTIAN. Sue. My mother. The lady who took your baby into the kitchen. *(smiles)* I'm sure he's safe.

YOUNG WOMAN. That's your mother?

BASTIAN. Sue.

YOUNG WOMAN. Funny. You don't look like Thom at all.

BASTIAN. Hilarious. I'm not Thom. I'm Bastian. Why would I look like–? How do you know about Thom?

YOUNG WOMAN. *(smiles)* I think I will sit down for a minute.

(**YOUNG WOMAN** *removes and drops her coat on the floor, revealing an outfit meant for someone of experience.*)

(**BASTIAN** *goes for the coat.*)

BASTIAN. Anyway, I'm Bastian.

YOUNG WOMAN. Unusual.

BASTIAN. It's French for adopted.

YOUNG WOMAN. No, it isn't.

BASTIAN. So. I'm Bastian.

YOUNG WOMAN. My feet are killing me.

BASTIAN. That was my mother Sue.

(**YOUNG WOMAN** *removes a shoe–a red patent leather pump.*)

BASTIAN. My sister Rissa–

RISSA. *(offstage)* Mother!

BASTIAN. Probably shouldn't see those shoes. What did you say your name was?

YOUNG WOMAN. Abigail.

BASTIAN. Abigail.

ABIGAIL. It's a horrible name.

BASTIAN. You should think about changing it.

ABIGAIL. To something more sophisticated?

BASTIAN. Like Constance.

ABIGAIL. Nice.

BASTIAN. You'll have to dye your hair.

ABIGAIL. I like it–

ABIGAIL/BASTIAN. "Constance."

(They are temporarily lost in each other's smile.)

ABIGAIL. No. I take it back. In this light, you do look like Thom.

*(**RISSA** descends the stairs, appearing now to be about six months pregnant.)*

RISSA. Mother, that may be my brother upstairs, but I tell you what; he looks absolutely nothing like Bastian. And he wouldn't lift one finger to help me find my–

BASTIAN. Red patent leather pumps?

*(**RISSA** notices **ABIGAIL** on the sofa. In a long, tense pause, **RISSA** takes in **ABIGAIL** in her entirety–especially her shoes.)*

RISSA. Who. The hell. Are you?

BASTIAN. Abigail!

ABIGAIL. You must be–

RISSA. *(vehemently)* Constance.

ABIGAIL. I thought her name was "Rissa".

RISSA. Maybe it is, and maybe it isn't.

ABIGAIL. Sorry to barge in like this on Thanksgiving.

RISSA. After all of these years.

ABIGAIL. I didn't have anywhere else to go.

RISSA. Abigail, Abigail, Abigail.

ABIGAIL. It's horrible; I know.

RISSA. Maybe you should change it.

BASTIAN. She has.

RISSA. To what?

ABIGAIL/BASTIAN. Constance.

RISSA. Constance is a loose girl's name.

*(**ABIGAIL** smiles knowingly.)*

RISSA. Those are some nice shoes you've got there. Very nice. What color would you say they were?

ABIGAIL. Red.

RISSA. Shiny.

ABIGAIL. Patent leather.

RISSA. Two inch?

ABIGAIL. Three.

RISSA. Size?

ABIGAIL. Seven.

RISSA. Bastian's a nine. Aren't those nice shoes, Bastian?

BASTIAN. I really didn't notice.

RISSA. Bastian has an affinity for red patent leather pumps.

BASTIAN. She's lying.

RISSA. I'd keep a real tight grip on them if I were you.

ABIGAIL. The man at Mack's Resale Shop said they were vintage.

RISSA/BASTIAN. You bought them at Mack's?

ABIGAIL. The resale shop on–

BASTIAN/ABIGAIL. Bluebonnet and Main.

RISSA/ABIGAIL. Next to the football field.

RISSA/BASTIAN. We know!

RISSA. I wonder how they got there.

BASTIAN. Mother.

RISSA/BASTIAN. Wretched woman.

ABIGAIL. I thought maybe they belonged to a movie star or something.

RISSA. Or something.

BASTIAN. Not many movie stars pass through Easton.

ABIGAIL. Not much of anything passes through Easton. Except Thom.

RISSA. What movie star do you think they belonged to, Bastian?

BASTIAN. Clark Gable.

ABIGAIL. I just meant they're old, the shoes. And all old things have stories.

RISSA. Did you hear that, Bastian?

BASTIAN. I'm standing right here.

RISSA. "All old things have stories."

BASTIAN. Mother's full of them.

RISSA. What is she?

BASTIAN. A hundred and seven by now.

> (**RISSA** *and* **BASTIAN** *erupt in laughter.* **ABIGAIL** *joins in, as the other two stop. Awkwardness.*)

ABIGAIL. I wonder what story these shoes have to tell.

BASTIAN. Riss?

RISSA. Maybe those shoes don't want to tell you their story.

BASTIAN. Maybe you should tell us your story.

ABIGAIL. I'm not good with stories.

BASTIAN. We're still not certain why you're here.

ABIGAIL. I just came to drop something off. I should be going.

> (**MOTHER** *enters.* **RISSA** *feels the presence of the baby before seeing it.*)

RISSA. Mother, put that thing down! Drop that thing at once!

MOTHER. Just because he arrived first, there's no need to throw a tantrum.

RISSA. There's no need to throw that baby out the window either, but for some reason I want to. Are you responsible for this?

ABIGAIL. Half responsible.

RISSA. How careless. I think mothers should take *full* responsibility for their children.

ABIGAIL. Not all women should be mothers.

RISSA. Of course they should. It's our god-given right.

MOTHER. It's our god-given obligation.

BASTIAN. It's not like men can be mothers.

RISSA. So that only leaves us.

ABIGAIL. Not all women want to be mothers.

MOTHER/RISSA. Don't they?

RISSA. Are you a lesbian?

BASTIAN. Rissa.

RISSA. What? Lesbians are women who don't want to be mothers.

BASTIAN. That's not true.

RISSA. Apparently they don't want to be mothers if they don't want to fuck men.

MOTHER. And some women don't have a choice in the matter. *(re: "fuck")* What did you just say??

RISSA. How old are you?

ABIGAIL. Sixteen.

BASTIAN. With a baby?

MOTHER. Maybe she's a loose girl, like that Constance.

BASTIAN. I think she is Constance.

MOTHER. I've a good mind to talk to your parents, young lady.

RISSA. Tell them she's a lesbian.

MOTHER. What's their imaginary number?

BASTIAN. You should've gotten out when you had the chance.

RISSA. She's so young. She probably doesn't even know what a lesbian is. It happens all the time with girls her age. They don't discover it until they're in college.

MOTHER. I never went to college.

ABIGAIL. I know what a lesbian is.

RISSA. And?

ABIGAIL. I'm pretty sure I'm not one.

RISSA. Yet. Give it time. My mother's a lesbian.

MOTHER. I am?

BASTIAN. No, she isn't.

RISSA. Isn't she?

MOTHER. Am I?

BASTIAN. No.

RISSA. That sure is a big baby. Mother, was I a big baby?

BASTIAN. You still are.

RISSA. What do we call a baby like that? A baby so big?

MOTHER. We haven't been properly introduced. I've just been calling him fish baby. Maybe we should call him Martin.

BASTIAN. Why? Is he drunk?

MOTHER. He should be by now.

RISSA. I think we should call him Quasimodo. And lock him in a bell tower, so he doesn't frighten all the other little children.

MOTHER. I vote for Martin.

BASTIAN. I vote for fish baby.

RISSA. Yes, that sure is a big baby. My baby's going to be bigger than your baby. He'll be bigger than all of us and will kick your baby's ass if he wants to. I'll tell him not to fight; it's the right thing to do. But since he'll be bigger than me, I probably won't be able to stop him. And being so big, he'll probably only have to hit your baby once.

MOTHER. Fish baby will just have to learn how to duck.

ABIGAIL. When is your baby due?

RISSA. Any minute now.

MOTHER. *(quietly to baby)* Isn't that right?

RISSA. I was shooting for seven o'clock-ish.

MOTHER. *(same)* Fishy, fishy baby.

ABIGAIL. Shouldn't you be at the hospital?

RISSA. Why? I'm not sick.

MOTHER. *(same)* Ah-boo.

BASTIAN. OK! No more baby talk!

(**MOTHER**, *who was "cooing," stops.*)

No more talking about babies, pregnancies or anything else!

MOTHER. Bastian, I've never seen you so animated.

RISSA. I really wish you'd stop screaming!

MOTHER. I think it's nice!

RISSA. It won't be nice when he deafens my baby. Jacques will have little or no play dates if he's deaf. All of his friends will think he's a snob for ignoring them. They'll be saying "Red rover, red rover, let Jacquie come over." Poor little Jacques will still be on the merry-go-round unable to hear their requests.

MOTHER. Maybe your baby is deaf, too, Connie.

RISSA. See what you did, Bastian? Now Quasimodo's deaf.

(**BASTIAN** *pulls* **ABIGAIL** *by the arm.*)

BASTIAN. There is a strange man upstairs in my mother's bed.

MOTHER. There isn't a strange man in my bed.

BASTIAN. Would you like to meet him?

ABIGAIL. Let's go, Bass.

MOTHER. It's simply their brother. Thom.

BASTIAN. How the hell is he our brother?

ABIGAIL. Thom? Here?

BASTIAN. How do you know Thom?

RISSA. Who the hell is Thom?

MOTHER. Your brother.

RISSA. I thought your name was Bastian.

BASTIAN. It is!

ABIGAIL. Tell him I'm here. Thom? Thom!

RISSA. Stop screaming! It won't do you any good. That man in mother's bed is dead to the world. Drunk as a skunk.

ABIGAIL. Thom doesn't drink.

RISSA. Really? Neither does she.

(*Everyone turns to notice* **MOTHER** *licking the bottom of her martini glass.*)

BASTIAN. Why am I the last person to meet this guy?

RISSA. I tried to meet him a few minutes ago; he just ignored me. At first I thought it was Daddy. He looks like Daddy, only younger. In fact, he looks like me, now that I think of it. We've the same earlobes. Mother, is that man upstairs my brother?

MOTHER. Thom. I've been trying to tell you all evening.

BASTIAN. I think it's time Thom wakes up. *(exits upstairs)*

ABIGAIL. I can't believe he's here. Give me the baby.

RISSA. You think I would've remembered having a brother named Thom.

MOTHER. He only showed up ten months ago.

RISSA. What does my baby brother have to do with you?

MOTHER. Thom is your older brother.

RISSA. Now, I'm just utterly confused. I need to sit down.

MOTHER. I need a drink.

RISSA. I need a drink, and I need to sit down.

MOTHER. The baby and I just finished off the martinis.

RISSA. So make some tequila slammers.

MOTHER. Excellent idea.

RISSA. No salt for me. My ankles are swollen.

MOTHER. Bastian's old tap shoes will never fit you now. *(exits)*

RISSA. My days in show business are over. *(pause)* So. Just who the hell are you?

*(**ABIGAIL** smiles and exits the window. **RISSA** exits the front door in pursuit of her shoes.)*

(banging from upstairs)

BASTIAN. *(offstage)* Who the hell are you???

*(**MOTHER** enters, carrying a tray with tea service, a bottle of tequila, and the baby atop it. She settles in for story time, occasionally doing a shot.)*

MOTHER. Once upon a time, there was a boy named "Sue". That isn't right. *(shot)* Once upon a time, there was a homecoming queen named "Sue," who wore nothing but lime green taffeta dresses. She was married to a tall, handsome, sober king named Martin, who fell in love with her rabbit stew. One evening, while enjoying a piping hot bowl, the castle bell rang. It was the mailman with a navy blue package addressed to Queen Sue, in care of King Martin. The package sat on the table until every last drop of the stew was gone and then like a jack-in-the-box, the package flew open and out came a bouncing baby boy. King Martin said, "We shall call him Prince Thomas Fuller of Sunflower Lane, and send–" *(pause)* "And send him out into the world to kill evil doers who press upon the Kingdom of Easton." King Martin placed Prince Thom back into the box, sealed it with many kisses, took a stamp from the bureau, and threw the box with all of his might high into the heavens. *(shot)* Ten months later, the mailman delivered another package addressed to Queen Sue. King Martin was away battling the Weeds and the armies of Ants, so Sue opened the red, patent leather box, and out rolled a big, fat baby girl. And Sue said, "I shall call you Princess Rissa Fuller, and hide you away from the evil doers of Easton, and you shall never leave my side." Sue even hid her from King Martin as best she could. Three years later, King Martin decided they needed a child in order to keep the kingdom from collapsing, so Sue brought out the red box, and introduced him to Princess Rissa. King Martin said princesses were of little use in battling weeds and ants, and that they'd have to wait for the arrival of a son. Except– *(beat)* Except no packages were ever delivered to that castle again. So. So, one day during battle, King Martin usurped a pink box, containing a baby boy from a neighboring kingdom. When King Martin returned home, he threw the box on the table next to the rabbit stew, looked at the Queen and said, "This'll do." *(shot)* Queen Sue loved both of her packages more than anything in the world, but was never quite able to stop looking to the high heavens, waiting for the day that her first box, containing the warrior Prince

Thom, fell down from the sky and back into her arms. Sue was lucky to have King Martin; she would've never had the strength to throw Thom's box up so high. Or to battle the neighboring kingdom for Prince Bastian. *(beat)* Maybe she would have. She probably had the strength of ten Martins inside her. Yes. I could be just like Martin. *(to baby)* You could be just like Martin. Yes, you could. All we'd need is another bottle of scotch. *(exits)* And a weed eater. *(gone)*

(RISSA chases ABIGAIL through the front door.)

RISSA. How much do you want for those shoes?

ABIGAIL. They're not for sale.

RISSA. I'll give you ten bucks. *(beat)* All right, for each.

BASTIAN. *(entering)* He's locked the door, and he won't come out.

ABIGAIL. Did you tell him I was here?

RISSA. Maybe that's why he won't come out. Bastian, where's your purse? I need to borrow twenty bucks.

(BASTIAN is sifting through the bureau.)

What are you doing?

BASTIAN. Looking for Dad's tools.

RISSA. Why?

BASTIAN. To build Jacques a tree house in the backyard. Where's Mother?

RISSA. She and Quasimodo are making tequila slammers.

(BASTIAN exits upstairs with tools.)

The backyard is that way.

ABIGAIL. What are you going to do with those tools?

RISSA. The question is, "What am *I* going to do with *you?*" That. Is the question.

ABIGAIL. What. Is the answer?

RISSA. Kick. Your. Ass.

ABIGAIL. What?

RISSA. If you're not going to give them those shoes, I'm just going to have to kill you.

(**RISSA** *chases* **ABIGAIL** *around the room.*)

ABIGAIL. What're you doing?

RISSA. About to kick your sweet ass, Abigail-Constance.

ABIGAIL. Thom!

RISSA. I'll let you throw the first punch, you big baby.

ABIGAIL. You're pregnant.

RISSA. Shut up, and hit me!

MOTHER. *(entering with tequila service)* Tequila slammers?

RISSA. Ooh. How nice. *(to* **ABIGAIL***)* I'm not through with you, Junior.

MOTHER. Where's Bastian?

RISSA. Building a nursery or something. I'll take his.

(*We hear banging upstairs.*)

MOTHER. What is that noise?

RISSA. Must be a southerly.

BASTIAN. *(offstage)* Ow! Shit!

MOTHER. I've never seen him to be so animated.

ABIGAIL. Sue.

(**MOTHER** *looks at* **RISSA.**)

RISSA. *She's* talking to you.

ABIGAIL. When did Thom get into town?

MOTHER. What is today?

RISSA. Tuesday.

ABIGAIL. Thursday.

MOTHER. Thom arrived on Tuesday.

ABIGAIL. Why didn't he find me?

MOTHER. Priorities?

ABIGAIL. Did he mention me?

MOTHER. To?

RISSA. Whom?

ABIGAIL. You?

MOTHER. When?

ABIGAIL. Ever?

MOTHER. What's your name again?

ABIGAIL. Abigail.

MOTHER. Name sounds familiar, but not from Thom. Weren't you Bastian's friend when he was five?

ABIGAIL. I'm Thom's friend.

RISSA. Abigail was my friend first!

(**BASTIAN** *descends the stairs with a pained look on his face and his hand wrapped in a dingy cloth.*)

MOTHER. How's the nursery coming, dear?

BASTIAN. I sliced my hand open on the–the–

MOTHER. Are you going to cry?

RISSA. I might cry, Mommy.

(**ABIGAIL** *sneaks upstairs.*)

BASTIAN. He won't come out.

RISSA. Was it easy for you to come out? *(about her belly)* These birthing things take time.

BASTIAN. I'm talking about Thom.

RISSA. Oh, Thom, Thom, Thom! I'm so sick of everyone talking about this Thom all the time. Can someone please pay attention to me for a change? I'm the one with the swollen ankles.

MOTHER. Tequila slammer?

RISSA. Please. But no more talking about Thom. Where's Constance?

(**ABIGAIL** *appears, as if upstairs.*)

(**MOTHER** *and* **BASTIAN** *freeze.*)

(**RISSA** *stays slightly active as* **ABIGAIL** *speaks to* **THOM** *outside the locked door.*)

ABIGAIL. Thom? It's Abigail. Abigail Fairchild. Remember me? Of course, you do; what am I saying? Open the door; it's Abigail. *(beat)* Actually, I go by Constance now, but you shouldn't remember that; I only changed it today. It was your brother's idea. You two look nothing alike. I'll change it back if you want. Did you get my letters? I wrote every day like you asked. I'm sure you were too busy killing foreign people in those far-off places to write back, but I hope you got mine. I tried sending you pictures of me, that way we talked about, but my father found them before I could get them in the mail. He only hit me once.

(**ABIGAIL** *and* **RISSA** *make eye contact, briefly.*)

I ran away. For a while. But then I found out I was... Anyway. I had to come. Funny; I had no idea you were back in town. No idea you were even going to be here when I dropped by. I was only stopping by to drop something off. But then your mother told me you were here, and now they *insist* that I stay for dinner. Isn't that something? *(beat)* Will you just open the fucking door???

(*Lights shift back to the living room.*)

RISSA. What's that wrapped around your hand?

BASTIAN. I found it in your old room.

RISSA. What have I told you about wearing my things?

(**RISSA** *rips the "cloth" from* **BASTIAN**'s *hand. She shakes it out, revealing a blood-stained dress. She is horrified, or confused.*)

This is my–*(pause)* You–*(beat)* There's blood on it.

(*She rushes out the front door.*)

MOTHER. Tequila slammer?

(*Lights shift back to* **ABIGAIL**. *Mother freezes.* **BASTIAN** *remains slightly active as* **ABIGAIL** *continues.*)

ABIGAIL. Let's see. What else is new? I have a birthday coming up. You probably do, too. Are you going to come out of there? You're sister said you were drunk. It's like she doesn't even know you. I told her you didn't drink unless someone has died. I hope no one has died.

(**ABIGAIL** *and* **BASTIAN** *make eye contact, briefly.*)

ABIGAIL. *(cont.)* Look, if you're avoiding your family, I can definitely see why; just let me in and we'll sneak out the window. Are you just tired from the war? Is that it? I bet that's it. Keep sleeping. I can wait. If you don't mind. I'll write you a letter for when you wake up. You do remember me. Don't you?

(Lights shift back to the living room. **ABIGAIL** *is gone.* **BASTIAN** *heads to the front door.)*

MOTHER. How did your friend die?

BASTIAN. What?

MOTHER. Your best friend.

BASTIAN. Alex.

MOTHER. Yes. How did he–?

BASTIAN. A gunshot. To the head.

MOTHER. Just like your father.

BASTIAN. *(smiles)* Oh, Mother. Dad died in a lawn-mowing accident.

MOTHER. Oh, that's right. Think Rissa's at the football field by now?

BASTIAN. Not without those shoes.

MOTHER. Sorry about your loss.

BASTIAN. Sorry about yours.

MOTHER. A gunshot.

BASTIAN. To the head.

MOTHER. That reminds me. He left you something.

BASTIAN. Alex?

MOTHER. Your father. *(***MOTHER** *slowly retrieves the box hidden under the sofa.)* I was going to wrap it and save it for Christmas, but I see no reason to make you wait. Who knows the next time we'll–

(She hands the box to a wary **BASTIAN**.*)*

Don't tell, Rissa.

BASTIAN. *(reading)* To Bass. Love Dad. Your handwriting.

MOTHER. I shot him and I'd do it again.

(**BASTIAN** *looks to* **MOTHER**. **MOTHER** *slowly looks away. Lights blink. It is one second before.*)

BASTIAN. *(repeat)* To Bass, Love Dad. Your handwriting.

MOTHER. His thoughts.

(**BASTIAN** *opens the box and slowly reveals a gun. Long silence.*)

(**RISSA** *enters the front door, wearing the blood-stained dress. She now appears to be legitimately pregnant.*)

RISSA. What'd I miss?

(**BASTIAN** *quickly hides the gun back in the box.*)

ABIGAIL. *(entering)* Thom should be down shortly.

MOTHER. I'll decide when Thom comes down. I'm the Mother.

BASTIAN. Then decide that he comes down now.

ABIGAIL. He's sleeping.

MOTHER. He'll be down for dinner.

RISSA. *(to stomach)* Since I'm your Mother, I've decided you'll come down *after* dinner. Ow! Don't you talk back to me.

ABIGAIL. He insisted I stay for dinner.

MOTHER. Did he?

RISSA. She can eat at the kid's table. *(to stomach)* What's that? I should wash your mouth out with soap.

BASTIAN. *(vacant)* I should wash up for dinner. *(heads for stairs)*

MOTHER. Bastian–

(**BASTIAN** *turns to* **MOTHER**, *who can't seem to find words; he continues upstairs.* **RISSA** *rubs her belly, staring at* **ABIGAIL**.*)

ABIGAIL. What's that on your dress?

RISSA. Love.

(Soft knocking from upstairs.)

BASTIAN. *(offstage)* Thom? It's–

MOTHER. Bastian?

(A loud gunshot.)

ABIGAIL. Thom?

(Another loud gunshot, as **RISSA** *grabs her stomach in pain.* **ABIGAIL** *runs upstairs. Baby cries from the kitchen.)*

MOTHER. *(vacant)* I must've left Quasi in the dish drainer. I'm so glad he cried before dinner. *(exits to kitchen)*

RISSA. I'm so glad somebody noticed I was shot!

*(***ABIGAIL** *screams from upstairs.* **RISSA** *stumbles to the sofa and drops dead.)*

ABIGAIL. *(offstage)* Thom? Thom! Bastian, what have you done?!

(Lights shift. **ABIGAIL**, **BASTIAN** *and* **MOTHER** *take the stage one at a time.)*

*(***ABIGIAL** *sits in a chair.* **BASTIAN** *stands, staring out the window, with the gun in hand.* **MOTHER** *finds her place.* **RISSA** *remains dead on the sofa.)*

*(***THOM**, *in formal military dress, enters through the wall, removing his hat. He circles the living room, taking the others in, before finally addressing the audience.)*

THOM. I was on leave when I heard Marty had died. A lawn-mowing accident up the road in Easton? I'd already buried two parents, so one more wasn't going to be that difficult. Especially one I hardly even knew. I borrowed my buddy's car to make the trip, and I remember feeling weird the whole way down. About meeting these people, who lived twenty minutes from where I grew up, and yet whom I'd never met. And still yet, who were my own flesh and blood. How many brothers or sisters did I have? I'd had none up until then. Were they going to look like me? Were they going to like me? My anxiousness caused me to pull into Thom's Liquor Store, just outside of Easton city limits. I have no idea why, I didn't even drink, but I walked into that store, grabbed two pints of scotch--or perhaps they were bourbon–and threw cash on the counter. The guy at the register asked where I was headed as he placed the bottles into brown sacks. I told him to Martin Fuller's funeral over in Easton. The man looked at me, shaking his head. Tears began to well in his eyes. "He was a fine, fine man, that Marty. I'm sorry for your loss," he said. Then he asked if I was of any relation. I said, "No. He simply cared for our lawn." Which was both true and a lie. I didn't want to bore him with details and I was already twenty minutes late for the funeral by that point. But I sure was grateful that he refused to take my money for the scotch or bourbon. He saluted me on my way out. And thanked me for protecting his country. I opened a bottle as soon as I got into the car. And had finished it by the time I ran into the sign at the funeral home. I was saddened, perhaps drunk, when I discovered there were no brothers or sisters waiting for me. Once again, I was the only child. The entirety of the funeral party consisted of me and Sue. Marty's wife? Mom. She looked exactly as I thought she would, except wearing a lime-green taffeta dress. Not typically fitting for a funeral. After our introductions, she immediately grabbed me and held me for what seemed an eternity. And then we went to the cemetery for the burial.

(**MOTHER** *begins to softly laugh.*)

As they lowered Marty into the ground, there must have been a crane malfunction, because Marty ended up caddy-corner to the burial plot. Stuck and immobile. We stood there for half an hour, while the workers mapped out a strategy for removal. Then Sue politely turned to me and asked if I would cry–

MOTHER. *(echo)* Would you cry?

THOM. Out loud.

MOTHER. *(echo)* Out loud?

THOM. I don't know if it was out of obligation to this woman for losing her husband, or simply the scotch, but I began to wail. Loudly and uncontrollably. She smiled.

MOTHER. Thank you.

THOM. And thanked me. And then said she had to be going.

MOTHER. *(echo)* I have to be going.

THOM. Something about looking into joining a gym. But she did say I was welcome to stay the night. If I didn't have to "rush back off to war." She gave me the address.

MOTHER. *(exiting)* 1-3-0-9 Sunflower Lane.

THOM. And then she walked away.

> (**MOTHER** *is gone.*)

I just stood there. Wailing. *(beat)* Ten months later, I will be killed while serving your country. But. Three hours later, I will meet a sweet girl named Abby.

> (**ABIGAIL** *stands and exits upstairs, sharing a knowing glance with* **THOM**.)

Who I will spend an entire evening with.

> (**ABIGAIL** *is gone.*)

Intimately. Which struck me as odd, because up to that point...

> (**THOM** *has made his way to the window.* **BASTIAN** *shifts. The two make a connection in silence, as the gun moves from* **BASTIAN**'s *hand to* **THOM**'s.)

I always thought I was gay.

> (**BASTIAN** *is gone.* **THOM** *notices a dead* **RISSA**. **THOM** *raises the gun to his chin.*)

Protecting an entire country can really get to a guy after a while.

> (*He lowers the gun and exits through the walls. He raises the gun to his eye.*)

Among other things.

(**THOM** *is gone. Two loud gunshots.*)

ABIGAIL. *(offstage)* Thom? Thom! Bastian, what have you done?

(*Lights up, action ensues.* **ABIGAIL** *rushes down the stairs.* **MOTHER** *enters with the baby.*)

ABIGAIL. Thom's dead!

MOTHER. Again? *(gasps)* Bastian?

(**BASTIAN** *enters with the gun.*)

BASTIAN. I'm right here.

MOTHER. My son.

THOM. *(entering from upstairs)* I'm right here.

MOTHER. My sons!

BASTIAN. I'm–

MOTHER. Make some room on the sofa, Riss. Rissa, move!

BASTIAN. You–?

ABIGAIL. You shot Thom.

MOTHER. No, he didn't. *(to* **BASTIAN***)* Did you?

RISSA. *(still dead)* He shot me.

BASTIAN. I shot the door handle to get in! But—

RISSA. Oh. When's dinner? Jacques's hungry.

BASTIAN. Mother, what is he doing here?

MOTHER. Not much of anything now.

(*All life leaves* **THOM** *It is a slight expiration; he is now "dead" on the sofa.*)

BASTIAN. He's dead.

RISSA. More for us. When do we eat?

MOTHER. Now's as good a time as any. Who wants to hold Quasi-Martin?

ABIGAIL. I want to hold Thom.

BASTIAN. Stop calling him that.

MOTHER. I'm sure he won't mind, though he's incapable of holding you back.

ABIGAIL. What the fuck did you do to him?

MOTHER. Gave birth is all I remember, and mind your language.

RISSA. I thought we were dispensing with the Thommy-talk. It's going to cause me to miscarry. *(to stomach)* Only kidding, bunny.

MOTHER. Rissa, don't be crass in front of our guest.

RISSA. *(to* ABIGAIL*)* Are you still here?

MOTHER. I meant your new brother. Rissa, this is Thom.

RISSA. Max who?

MOTHER. Say "hello," Riss.

RISSA. Make him say it first.

BASTIAN. He can't.

RISSA. Then neither can I.

BASTIAN. He's dead!

ABIGAIL. Stop calling him that!

BASTIAN. Mother, what's going on?

MOTHER. Thanksgiving! Thom, this is your younger brother Bastian.

RISSA. He's adopted.

MOTHER. My children usually aren't this rude. I guess you already know Abigail-Constance. (Slut.) Though, I'm still not quite sure how. *(whispers to Thom)* If you were still alive, I'd do my best to keep you away from the likes of her, but what's the worst she can do to you now? Bastian, I need your help getting a few things from the shed. Rissa, I need you to go into the kitchen and tray the turkey.

BASTIAN. Rissa!?

RISSA. I heard her!

MOTHER. I think we'll eat Thanksgiving dinner in here this year. Thom seems to take so well to all the light this room now provides without the curtains.

BASTIAN. I think we should re-hang the curtains.

MOTHER. Why?

BASTIAN. So no one sees in.

MOTHER. What are you ashamed of?

BASTIAN. There's a dead body on the sofa. Something for which I'm quite sure our neighborhood is not zoned.

MOTHER. Rissa will help me re-hang the curtains after dinner. Now, come with me to the shed.

RISSA. I have to give birth after dinner, Sue.

MOTHER. Then maybe little Jacques will lend us a hand.

BASTIAN. Explain to me what is going on!

MOTHER. First, help me in the shed.

RISSA. Yeah, Bastian. Help her in the shed.

(**BASTIAN** *points the gun at* **RISSA.**)

BASTIAN. Fuck the shed!

(**RISSA** *grabs the gun.*)

MOTHER. Rissa!

RISSA. Bastian said "fuck!"

MOTHER. What have I told you about guns?

RISSA. They're for boys?

(**BASTIAN** *grabs the gun from* **RISSA.**)

Then why does Bastian get to hold it?

MOTHER/BASTIAN. Because Bastian has more of a use for it.

RISSA. Drama queens.

BASTIAN. (*points gun at* **RISSA**) Pot! (*points gun at* **MOTHER**) Kettle!

MOTHER. I've about had it with both of you. CUT YOUR SHIT OR YOU'RE BOTH GROUNDED! That sounded just like Martin.

RISSA. Must be the scotch.

BASTIAN. You can't ground us!

RISSA. Not me; I'm thirty-five. You on the other hand–

MOTHER. Both of you! Bastian, outside. Rissa, march into that kitchen, put the turkey on a tray, and bring it back in here so we can sit down and enjoy a nice family dinner.

BASTIAN. How are we supposed to enjoy a nice family dinner like this?

RISSA/MOTHER. Fake it!

RISSA. That's what I plan to do.

MOTHER. Outside. Now!

BASTIAN. We're just going to leave them here?

MOTHER. Abigail-Constance apparently needs a little alone time with your brother.

RISSA/MOTHER. Slut.

MOTHER. And if we don't eat soon, we're going to waste away and blow off with the next southerly.

BASTIAN. How can you expect us to eat at a time like this?

MOTHER. It's nearly seven-thirty.

RISSA. I'm famished.

BASTIAN. And how the hell is this considered a family dinner? With some strange lady with some strange baby? And this–this–this fucking dead body sitting on our couch!

(**MOTHER** *slaps* **BASTIAN** *forcefully across the face. Silence.* **RISSA** *chuckles.* **MOTHER** *looks at* **RISSA**, *who cowers.*)

RISSA. Let's go tray the turkey, Quasi.

(**RISSA** *exits to the kitchen with a calculating smile.*)

MOTHER. I'll explain everything to you outside.

(*She waits for* **BASTIAN** *to exit. She grabs the gun from him, places it on the bureau, and then follows him out.*)

(*Lights shift.* **ABIGAIL** *addresses the audience.*)

ABIGAIL. I was coming out of Mack's Resale Shop on Bluebonnet and Main when I saw him for the first time. I had just bought a pair of shoes, having talked Mack down from twenty bucks to ten. I wasn't wearing a bra that day, which helped, but I sure was happy to walk out of that shop wearing red patent leather pumps. Anyway, he was dressed in his Winter Blues and a pea coat. He looked like a cross between Johnny Cash and James Dean, neither of whom I could picture in my mind at the time, and neither of whom I remember ever seeing cry the way he was crying when he passed by. I liked the way he smelled, so I followed him for several blocks. This was irritating, because we ended up right back at the football field, which was directly across the street from Mack's. My feet were beginning to hurt, but I had to find out who he was, and what he was doing in Easton.

(**MOTHER** *and* **BASTIAN** *appear side stage.* **MOTHER** *walks toward the shed;* **BASTIAN** *remains behind.*)

MOTHER. Apparently he discovered we were living in Easton, and he made his way down here for your father's funeral ten months ago. You could've met him then, but apparently you two had better places to be than your father's funeral. *(gone)*

ABIGAIL. The sun was going down, which cast a purple hue across the field. But there he was, sitting dead–dead center on the fifty yard line. I felt both nervous and excited; I felt like Cinderella in my red patent leather pumps, meeting my Prince Charming, Johnny-James, for the first time. I did my best to glide across the field in my new heels as they dug deeper and deeper into the dirt with each step. Eventually, I fell, but luckily, not before reaching the forty-ninth yard. I thought he was going to laugh; he just kept crying.

(**MOTHER** *enters carrying a shovel, overalls, and a weed eater. She makes her way to* **BASTIAN**, *handing him the shovel.*)

MOTHER. I was actually quite moved and quite pleased and quite surprised the way he cried so. It was totally unexpected. *(exits)*

(**RISSA** *appears from the kitchen.*)

ABIGAIL. I asked him why he was crying and he said his mother had asked him to. And then he took a big swig from a bottle of bourbon. He said he didn't drink and then he took another one. I asked if there was any-thing I could do, and then he immediately grabbed me and held me for what seemed an eternity. Then he began telling me his story. About his dead father, who was also their lawn boy? His years in the service. And some other sadness about having no siblings once again. By the end of it I found myself crying, too.

(**ABIGAIL** *laughs.*)

RISSA. How sad.

BASTIAN. Apparently, Dad made her give him away.

RISSA. Why did they need you?

ABIGAIL. He asked if he could kiss me. My first impulse was to say "No." But since his hand was already on my breast, I didn't see the point. So he kissed me. Eighteen times. I counted each and every one. It wasn't my first kiss, but it was my first time to taste bourbon. He said kissing me made him forget his sadness. I asked how he could be sad for someone he never really knew.

(**THOM** *awakens.* **MOTHER** *appears at the stairs.*)

Which I think made him angry.

MOTHER. And so he hit you?

RISSA. Only once.

ABIGAIL. The kisses were more enjoyable than asking ques-tions, so I let him fuck me. I let. Him fuck me. We did it five times. *(beat)* By the last time–

RISSA/ABIGAIL. There were no kisses.

ABIGAIL. I'm not exactly sure how important kisses really are during the fifth time, but I knew we were in love. Afterwards, I told him my name.

THOM/RISSA. Abby.

ABIGAIL. Strangely, no one had ever called me "Abby" before, and no one has since. He said his name was–

THOM/BASTIAN. Alex.

ABIGAIL. But asked that I call him–

THOM/MOTHER. Thom.

(**MOTHER** *makes her way to* **BASTIAN**.)

ABIGAIL. We noticed the sun was coming up, and Thom said he had to be going, because his mother was surely worried sick.

THOM/RISSA. Or–

ABIGAIL. That he had to return his buddy's car.

THOM/RISSA. Or–

ABIGAIL. That he had to rush back off to war.

RISSA. Or.

ABIGAIL. I told him I'd write to him every single day until we were together again. As long as he promised me not to get shot.

(**THOM** *shoots* **ABIGAIL** *with his finger and an audible wink.*)

ABIGAIL. He promised me with a wink.

(**THOM** *slowly makes his way to the door.*)

BASTIAN. Suicide.

MOTHER. The letter said "friendly fire."

BASTIAN. Same thing.

ABIGAIL. He didn't kiss me good-bye, or offer me a ride home, but he did say we should get married the next time he was in town.

(**THOM** *quickly exits the front door.*)

And that was enough.

RISSA. *(vehemently)* Liar!

ABIGAIL. That was enough.

BASTIAN. Suicide.

MOTHER. That's enough!

(*Lights shift.* **ABIGAIL** *exits upstairs.* **RISSA** *exits to the kitchen.*)

(**BASTIAN** *enters the front door with the shovel and leans it against the bureau.*)

BASTIAN. *(to no one)* Suicide.

(**RISSA** *enters with a large origami turkey on a tray.*)

RISSA. *(to no one)* Our dead brother is Quasimodo's father.

(**BASTIAN** *brandishes the gun.*)

BASTIAN. Suicide is just what you need.

(**MOTHER** *enters with the overalls.*)

MOTHER. What's that smell?

(**RISSA** *places the turkey on the sofa, pulling from it a large carving knife.*)

RISSA. I must've left fish baby in that pot on the stove.

(**RISSA** *exits upstairs, dragging the knife across the sofa.*)

(**BASTIAN** *exits to the kitchen with the gun.*)

(**MOTHER** *sits on the sofa and stares at the turkey.*)

(**THOM** *enters the front door with the weed eater on his shoulder.*)

MOTHER. *(to herself)* I don't think I want to be a mother anymore.

THOM. Try being a father.

(**THOM** *circles the living room, inspecting the carpet.*)

(**MOTHER**, *with a vague sense of clarity, begins to undress. She steps into the overalls.*)

(*At the end of* **MOTHER**'s *transformation, and* **THOM**'s *inspection, they meet together, shoulder to shoulder, holding the weed eater.*)

(**BASTIAN** *enters with the baby in a stew pot and the gun. He walks to* **MOTHER** *and touches her face.*)

THOM/BASTIAN. It's time I go.

MOTHER. I'm so glad.

(**BASTIAN** *exits the front door, with the gun and the baby in the pot.*)

MOTHER. I'm so glad you made it home for Thanksgiving.

THOM. I know.

(*THOM hands* MOTHER *the weed eater, grabs the shovel, and heads for the door.*)

MOTHER. Thom you know I–

THOM. I know.

(*THOM exits the front door, and walks to the window.* MOTHER *rushes to the window.*)

MOTHER. Thom! *(beat)* What am I going to do? About this carpet?

(*Lights begin to fade on* THOM.)

THOM. *(softly)* Care for it. *(gone)*

(*MOTHER grabs a bottle of scotch and begins to "water" the carpet.*)

(*RISSA slowly descends the stairs with the knife. She goes to the phone and speaks at it, not into it.*)

RISSA. Rosie, I'd like to report a murder.

(*ABIGAIL appears, giggling on the stairs.*)

(*BASTIAN appears side stage, holding the gun.*)

BASTIAN. Suicide is just what you need when you're home for the holidays.

RISSA. *(at phone)* I mean, suicide. Yes. No–you have a nice day.

(*RISSA lifts the receiver and places it beside the phone. We hear a faint dial tone. She exits upstairs after* ABIGAIL.)

(*MOTHER continues watering the perimeter of the room.*)

(*BASTIAN talks to the baby, who is still in the pot on the floor.*)

BASTIAN. Sorry you have to witness this.

(*Sounds of an approaching wind, along with the whispering voices from the beginning of the play. Both rise in volume. The phone moves from a dial tone to a faint beeping.*)

BASTIAN. *(cont.)* But look at it this way; you'll have a great story to tell your children. Oh, that's right. Boys can't have babies–

(**BASTIAN** *quickly raises the gun to his head. He panics, and is unable to pull the trigger. He lets out a guttural scream.*)

(*There is a different scream from upstairs [***RISSA***].*)

(**MOTHER** *is having her own release.*)

(*During the course of the various fits,* **ABIGAIL** *calmly rushes down the stairs. She is now wearing the blood-stained dress and is barefoot. She exits the window as the screams subside.*)

ABIGAIL. *(outside)* Bye. *(gone)*

(**RISSA** *appears on the stairs. She is dressed completely different–adult and no longer pregnant.*)

(*She holds her red patent leather pumps in her arms.*)

MOTHER. *(to the carpet)* Did you see that?

BASTIAN. *(to the baby)* Stupid baby!

RISSA. *(to the pumps)* Yes.

MOTHER. You grew!

RISSA. Yes!!!

BASTIAN. Stupid baby tell me a story. No–I'll tell you one. Once upon a time, your father's dead. *(laughs)*

(**MOTHER** *and* **RISSA** *each laugh for their own reasons.* **RISSA** *puts on the red, patent leather pumps.*)

Cheer up. I never knew either of mine; look how I turned out. That's not why I'm doing this. There's a whole world of information you will never know. A whole world of information that stories could never tell. And even if they could, who would listen?

MOTHER. *(ear to carpet)* Listen–

RISSA. Once upon a time...

MOTHER. You can almost hear it grow.

BASTIAN. Once upon a time, there was a boy named "Sue." I've just decided your name is Sue.

MOTHER. It's not much, but it's definitely a start.

BASTIAN. And he was stuck in a pot and left on the doorstep of a cryptic house. A house full of several stories.

RISSA. Stories.

BASTIAN. Several stories and a gun and–

RISSA. Babies.

BASTIAN. *(shift)* It makes perfect sense to me now why you'd want to kill yourself.

RISSA. Baby.

BASTIAN. Makes perfect, perfect, perfect, perfect, perfectly good sense to me that you must die. You do want me to shoot you, don't you Sue?

MOTHER. Yes–

(**RISSA** *laughs.*)

BASTIAN. All you have to do is say the word and I'll shoot.

MOTHER. It'll probably grow an inch or two before breakfast.

BASTIAN. Just say it.

RISSA. *(looking to the window)* Where's Quasi-Martin?

MOTHER. I'm done caring for Martin, and fish, and babies, too. From now on, I care for my carpet.

BASTIAN. Just say it!

RISSA. *(out the window)* Bastian!

(**BASTIAN** *looks to the audience as if at* **RISSA**.)

BASTIAN. Pinkies!

RISSA. Say "I love you."

MOTHER. Say it first.

RISSA. I–

BASTIAN. *(gun on baby)* I can't?

MOTHER. Neither can I.

BASTIAN. *(gun on baby)* But I will. *(gone)*

(RISSA *backs away from the window in her red pumps;* **MOTHER** *starts the weed eater and moves across the floor.*)

(*There is a deafening gunshot.* **MOTHER** *and* **RISSA** *stop, as does the weed eater.*)

(*The sound of the pot dropping.*)

(*Another deafening gunshot. The longest silence.*)

RISSA. Well–

MOTHER. Well.

RISSA. I'll be home before dark. *(goes to the window)*

MOTHER. It is dark.

(RISSA *deliberately shuts the window and locks it.*)

RISSA. Then I guess you shouldn't wait up for me.

(RISSA *exits the front door, leaving it wide open.*)

(**MOTHER** *sits on the floor with her weed eater and bottle of scotch.*)

MOTHER. I really am happy that all my children made it home for Thanksgiving. *(beat)* I wonder if they'll make it home for Christmas.

(*Faint sound of a baby crying in the distance; perhaps it's fish baby, perhaps it's not.*)

MOTHER. *(to carpet)* Shh. There, there now. There, there.

(*The lights slowly fade with a passing wind.*)

END OF PLAY.

PROPERTY LIST

Cleaning rag

Box for gun

Gun

Stationery

Pen

Emery board (file)

Phone

Tools (i.e., hammer, screwdriver, etc.)

Tequila bottle

Barbie Doll

Ken Doll

Flask

Scotch bottle

Christmas present(s)

Tap shoes

Bunny slippers

Hatbox

Various cocktail glasses (rocks, wine, champagne, etc.)

Weed eater

Pay phone receiver

Shovel

Serving tray for turkey

Tea tray for tequila service

Drink tray for mojito service

Drink tray for martini service

Martini service

Mojito service

Large origami turkey

Butcher knife

Stew pot

Baby doll

SOUND EFFECTS

Wind

Door bell

Baby crying

Gunshots

IN THE SAWTOOTHS

Dano Madden

Dramatic Comedy / 3m

Oby, Nellie and Darin have been friends since high school. No
in their thirties, they have become busier in their lives, but on
thing remains constant: their annual backpacking adventure i
the mountains of Idaho. As their trip nears and they have mad
all of the necessary preparations to survive in the outdoors, the
lives are suddenly shattered by tragedy. What ensues is a tru
test of an old friendship. Can Oby, Nellie and Darin remai
friends as they desperately try to navigate through an immens
and unexpected wilderness? *In the Sawtooths* was developed at th
Seven Devils Playwrights Conference in Idaho and at The Lar
Play Development Center in New York City.

In the Sawtooths *was the winner of the*
Kennedy Center's 2007 National Student Playwriting Award.

IT IS NO DESERT

Dan Stroeh

Drama / 1m / Bare stage

This moving account of the author's struggles against neurofibra-motosis, a progressively debilitating disease for which there is no cure, was performed at the Kennedy Center in Washington, D.C..

Winner! 2001 American College Theatre Festival Award

THE LAST SUPPER RESTORATION

Dan O'Brien

Drama / 4m, 1f / Interior

The deathbed delusions of Bob Sarafin, a contemporary New York shirt designer and artist manque, are portrayed in a dreamlike narrative that weaves the imagined story of Leonardo da Vinci with that of Sarafin's father, an art restorer in Milan during World War II. As the nucleus of contemporary characters, people who are close to Sarafin, are called on to inhabit an eclectic selection of historical figures ranging from Sigmund Freud to Ezra Pound, The Last Supper Restoration becomes a mediation on the power of secrecy, betrayal and the possibility for human transcendence. Performed at the Kennedy Center as part of the American College Theatre Festival, this innovative work won the 1997 National Student Playwriting Award and the National AIDS Fund/CDFA Vogue Initiative.

Winner! 2001 American College Theatre Festival Award

SOCIAL DARWINISM

Angela Gant

Comedy / 5m, 5f

Social Darwinism is an absurdist socio-political comedy that follows a familial group: an Alpha Male, Alpha Female, Second Banana, Subordinate Female, Adolescent Male, Adolescent Female, Outside Male, and Outside Female as they move through several different social classes. The plays looks at racism, male homosexuality, and feminist ideals. Additionally, Social Darwinism shows the subjugation of women, which changes as the play evolves.

Winner, 2006 Kennedy Center American College Theatre Festival National Student Playwriting Award

Winner, 2006 Paula Vogel Award Kennedy Center ACTF

"Gant finds new comedic ways to bare a number of societal sins that she is far from the first to protest against...There is no shortage of laugh-out-loud moments within playwright Angela Gant's original adult comedy *Social Darwinism*."
– *Lubbock Avalanche Journal*